MW01101733

Acclaim for Rod Norville's
MOONSHINE EXPRESS
With the History of Moonshine
Today and Yesterday

"Highly recommended and thoroughly enter-
taining as a wild and desperate saga of escape,
independence, and a struggle to survive."

Midwest Book Review

"Norville knows how to write good fiction, using spare words that hold meaning . . . The
plot moves lickety-split . . . The literary touches
here are wonderful, not only do you read this
book for the characters and the theme, but for
the writing.
Moonshine Express is compulsively readable
and lavishly imagined."

The Book Reader - America's most

independent reviewer

" An engaging story . . . a first-rate developing
action story . . . Norville's taut action takes the
time to explore the character's emotions."

Voya

". . . reminds me of *The Adventures of Huckle-
berry Finn.*"

Los Altos Town Crier

" *Moonshine Express* is based upon a youth-
ful experience of author Rod Norville . . . "

Amarillo Globe News

"*Moonshine Express* simply shines. I heard
echoes of Faulkner in Norville's view of the
South."

Kent Braithwaite - Author of
The Wonderland Murders

FEATURED ON:

"THE VOICE OF AMERICA Radio Network"
"NOONDAY SHOW" at WBTV-TV (CBS)-
Charlotte, NC
"THE MORNING SHOW" at WKMG-TV (CBS)-
Orlando, FL
"THE EARLY SHOW" at WCTV-TV (CBS)-
Tallahassee, FL
"THE MORNING SHOW" at WJXT-TV (CBS)-
Jacksonville, FL
'ROCKY DEE SHOW" at WTM-AM (CBS)-
Charleston, SC
"ANDY JOHNSON SHOW" at WJGR (CBS)-
Jacksonville, FL
"FROM THE HEART" Radio Show-
San Francisco/San Jose, CA

Moonshine Express

With a History of
Moonshine
Today and Yesterday

proper as top #15.

Moonshine Express

With a History of
Moonshine
Today and Yesterday

By Rod Norville

Four Seasons Publishers
Titusville, FL

Cougar Mountain Junior High School
5tLb 2:0th Street East
Graham, WA 98338

Moonshine Express
With a History of Moonshine Today and Yesterday

All rights reserved
Copyright©2003 Rod Norville

This is a work of fiction.
All characters and events portrayed in this book are
fictional, and any resemblance to real people is purely
coincidental.

Reproduction in any manner, in whole or in part,
in English or in other languages, or otherwise
without written permission of publisher is prohibited.

New Edition

For information contact: Four Seasons Publishers
P.O.Box 51, Titusville, FL 32781

PRINTING HISTORY
First Printing 2003

ISBN 1-891929-99-2

PRINTED IN THE UNITED STATES OF AMERICA
1 2 3 4 5 6 7 8 9 10

This book is dedicated to Margie and Katrina

Forward

You might think that moonshine-or the making of illegal liquor-went out of style with your Grandfather's Grandfather shortly after prohibition.. But the truth is plenty of bootleg whiskey is still being made today and, of course, its still a felony offense.

But that hasn't stopped the 139 people convicted in 19 states across the country, including California and New York, from being involved in moonshine-related activities during the last four-and–a-half years. **

Why would these people and others yet to be apprehended, risk possible conviction of a federal offense when so much legal liquor is readily available? I've attempted to answer that question in the following Prologue that includes the latest information available on our modern day "shiners. It also includes my own personal – and dangerous – encounter in the '50s with some very tough bootleggers about to make a "run", and a pertinent history of moonshine liquor from its Scottish-Irish immigration roots to locations where it is still going on today.

The only thing that isn't entirely true is my novel, which follows, "Moonshine Express". "Moonshine Express" is a family adventure story taking place in the swamps of northern Florida in the 50s and involves a vicious moonshiner intent upon killing two youngsters who stumble upon his whiskey still.

I want to thank my award winning former news reporter, Wendy Bailey< for interviewing the authorities who supplied information about current moonshine activities. I also want to thank the authors I've noted and several Internet articles. And a belated, but deeply sincere, thanks to the 'shiners who spared my life in the back-roads of Georgia one Moon-crossed night so many years ago.

I lived to write about it.

Rod Norville

** These statistics from the disclosure Division of the Alcohol, Tobacco, and Firearms Agency (ATF) in Washington, D.C. were gathered shortly before the date of publication of this book.

Prologue

The Latest Information Available on Today's Moonshiners

My Personal Brush with Moonshiners

History of Moonshine Today and Yesterday

The Latest Information Available on Today's Moonshiners

It may be hard to believe that with the shelves of your local liquor store fully stocked with the greatest variety of distilled spirits imaginable that anyone would want to be a moonshiner.

But, surprisingly enough, people do. Even today. And the arrests and convictions continue some 70 years after Prohibition when bootleggers were making news daily.

Since October of 1998, 139 people in 19 states across the U.S. were arrested in connection with moonshining activities. During that same period, 139 convictions followed as a result of investigations into alleged production of illegal liquor. Moonshine related arrests were conducted in the states of: Alabama, California, Florida, Georgia, Iowa, Kentucky, Maryland, Massachusetts, Michigan, New Jersey, New Mexico, New York, Ohio, Pennsylvania, Tennessee, Texas, Virginia, and Wyoming.

The highest number of moonshine-related apprehensions during that time took place in Virginia (29 arrests) ; Tennessee (25 arrests) ; New York (18 arrests) ; Georgia (17 arrests); and California (11 arrests). (Please refer to the chart at the end of the text.)

In fact, just since the beginning of 2002, there have been 37 arrests related to moonshine activities in six states across the country. Thirty-five convictions followed in the same time period.

You might ask yourself, as I did, why are people continuing to risk facing Federal Grand Jury felony charges in order to make their own distilled spirits? And why would anyone partake of another person's illegal activity-and possibly health-endangering-liquor?

Is it because it tastes good? Granddad's white lightning may have a unique flavor because it's made from a tried and true recipe handed down through generations, but it may also include toxic fluids such as wood alcohol and embalming fluid to give it more "kick". And these fluids can lead to paralysis, blindness, and even death. People aren't buying it for taste.

The real reason people drink and make moonshine is the same reason they did it years ago. MONEY. Big savings for the drinker and huge profits for the "shiner.

As Special Agent in Charge, Jeff Roehm of the Bureau of Alcohol, Tobacco, and Firearms (ATF) in Washington, D.C. told my reporter: "There is a huge profit motive in making moonshine even today. The bootleggers can keep literally all of the profits and not have to pay state or federal taxes."

Roehm went on to say that there are "nip" joints in Washington, D.C., Philadelphia, and Baltimore where (cheap) moonshine is sold under the counter.

He also said that million of dollars in state and federal tax revenues are lost each year to moonshining.

There's still a market for the 'shiners to fill and the feds are still trying to catch them. Just like they did in your Granddaddy's day.

More information follows about moonshining today and yesterday. I hope you enjoy it.

Moonshine Express

Persons Arrested or Convicted by State Involved in
"Moonshine" Activity - Courtesy of the
Disclosure Division of the Bureau of Alcohol,
Tobacco, and Firearms of the
Department of the Treasury

State	Oct. 1, 1998 to Mar. 12, 2003		Jan. 1, 2002 to Mar. 12, 2003	
	Arrested	Convicted	Arrested	Convicted
ALA	3	3		
CA	11	11		
FL	5	5		
GA	17	17	10	12
IOWA	4	4		4
KY	2	2	1	
MYLD	8	8		
MASS	2	2		
MICH	2	2		
MISSOURI	1	1	1	1
N.J	5	5		
N.MEX	1	1		
N.Y.	18	18	1	2
OHIO	1	1		
PA	1	1		
TENN	25	25	23	16
TX	2	2		
VA	29	29	1	
WY	2	2		
TOTAL	139	139	37	35

Rod Norville

My Personal Brush with Moonshiners

Crafton's faded white 1940 Chevy sedan with splotched gray primer covering a variety of dents sputtered, coughed and then coasted to a stop at the side of the road. Crafton exploded an expletive. Gray, sitting beside him said, "Ah Jeez, Crafton. Y'all ran outta gas."

I raised up from the back seat where I'd been sleeping. "Where are we?"

Crafton shoved back in his seat. "Probably 'bout 30 miles north of Atlanta, Norville."

I opened the rear door and stepped out into a humid Georgia evening. I looked up and down the asphalt two-lane road. It was dusk. No cars in sight in either direction. I leaned into Crafton's open window. "Pass any gas stations in the last few miles?"

"Not since we came through Atlanta."

"How far to the next town?"

Gray unfolded a wrinkled map. "Must be 10 miles or more."

Crafton exploded another expletive. "We won't be gettin' to Nashville tonight!"

I'd met Crafton and Gray shortly after being transferred into a Strategic Air Command Bomber base in Savannah, Georgia, a few months earlier. Crafton and Gray were both from Tennessee; Crafton from Nashville and Gray from the hill country. I was from an orange grove town next to the desert in Southern California.

Crafton had invited Gray and me to share expenses on a trip to Tennessee over our first long weekend. Crafton was anxious to see his 16-year-old Nashville wife, Anna Lee. He was my best buddy and I wanted to meet her. I didn't know Gray very well but felt protective toward him. He wanted to see his hill country girlfriend that he described as being very fat. "I got a lot more woman for lovin' than any of ya'll," he chuckled with averted eyes. I looked up the road. "Just a minute, there's a pickup truck comin'." I prepared to flag it down. Crafton and Gray jumped out and joined me. The pickup, a late 1940s Ford, suddenly slowed and turned onto a dirt path in a cloud of red Georgia dust and headed up into the hills. Crafton had another expletive for the occasion.

"Come on," I said and took off up the road.

"Where y'all goin', Norville?" Crafton yelled.

I broke into a trot. "That pickup is our only chance for gas." Crafton, medium height, raw-boned with a friendly but horsey-looking face, joined me. Gray, a skinny little guy with a face as gray as his name and a pronounced limp, tried to keep up.

Gray, like all of us, had enlisted at age 18 during the last year of the Korean war. During his first leave home, he'd gone 'coon huntin' with a 16-gauge shotgun and accidently shot a couple of toes off his right foot while climbing over a barbwire fence.

Popular wisdom in the Squadron said Basic Training had been such a cultural shock to Gray, he'd schemed on getting a quick medical discharge by blowing his toes off. Whatever, he didn't get a discharge and now trotting along, he looked a little like Dennis Weaver in his role as the gimp, Chester, in the '60's "Gunsmoke" TV series.

We were dressed in a mixed bag of uniform and civilian clothing: Air Force black brogan boots, black wool socks and black belt. Civilian faded levis and western shirts for Crafton and Gray and a short-sleeve California flower-print for me.

Dusk was turning into night as we slowed to a fast walk noting that a rickety wooden fence bordered one side of the path and scattered large stones bordered the other. The rolling hills on both sides of the path were covered in blue-green grass and Georgia pines of varying sizes. No houses, no people, an occasional cow. The night was quiet except for the rustle of little creatures as we disturbed them from going to bed or getting up for the night.

It was surreal as we kept climbing ever higher into the hills under a blanket of light from a rising full moon. We came around a final hill and saw the pickup truck parked by the front door of a rustic and unpainted farm house set back off the road.

Crafton stopped in his tracks. "I think we better get the hell outta here."

Gray nodded his agreement. A dozen 1939 and 1940 Fords were parked around the dirt yard.

"This is the only place we're gonna find any gas tonight," I said and stepped onto the front porch and knocked on the door. I heard some commotion inside and after a lengthy period of time, the door opened a crack. I could make out a tall man in blue bib overalls eyeing me. The door slowly opened the rest of the way and I saw a room full of similarly dressed country men now all standing and angrily staring at me.

Bouncing from one foot to the other, I said, "Hi, folks, we're in the service on our way to Nashville. We ran outta gas. Could we buy some from you?"

They clustered together and whispered a bit. I looked at Crafton and Gray. They were as forlorn as a couple of toothless coyotes in the California desert. After the longest tension period I'd had in my short life, the leader barked an order to the man closest to us, "Take 'em outside and guard 'em."

I was stunned. It dawned on me that these were the toughest looking dudes I'd ever encountered (Years later, I saw similar looking characters in the Burt Reynolds movie, "Deliverance").

The guard grabbed my shirt front and slammed me back onto

the porch.

I said, "What's going on?"

He closed the door.

"What're you doin'?"

He shook his head slowly at me as if to say, "Don't waste your breath, boy."

After a lifetime, the door opened and the leader waved the guard in and whispered something to him. It crossed my mind to run for it, but run from what, to where and why?

The guard came out, closed the door and without saying a word motioned for us to get into the cluttered bed of the pickup. We didn't need to be asked a second time.

The guard walked to an adjacent shed and came back with a can of gasoline and set it down in the bed beside us. A few minutes later, we pulled up along side the Chevy and the guard motioned for us to get out. We were out in a heart beat. Gray and Crafton poured gas while I stood beside the guard sitting behind the wheel.

"What do we owe you?" I asked. He stared at me.

"Well, anyhow, thanks, " I said. He continued staring.

Crafton put the cap back on the now empty can and set it shakily back into the bed of the pickup.

The guard stuck his head out his window, pointed up the road toward Nashville and spoke for the first time, "Now, y'all get you're asses outta heah and don't y'all never come back. Y'all heah?"

He sped away burning first gear rubber.

We jumped into the Chevy and heeded his advice, burning not only first gear rubber, but second and maybe a little third gear as well.

"Holy cow," I said.

"Crafton looked at me in the rear view mirror, "Norville, Ya'll just damn near got us kilt!"

"What do you mean, me?"

Gray answered, "They was moonshiners about to go on a run."

Crafton added, "They had to make a decision back there

whether to snuff and bury us in these hills or take the chance we'd blow the whistle on them with the first patrol car we saw."

Gray looked at Crafton, "It's a damn good thing Norville did the talkin' what with his California accent and all. They knew he warn't local."

"Holy cow," I said again.

A few years later, I read in a Reader's Digest article that the 1939 and 1940 Fords were the favorite vehicle for moonshiners transporting their 'shine in the '50s. There were several reasons; their flat-head V-8 engine could be easily souped-up with dual carburetors, milled heads and other modifications that allow speeds up to 100 miles per hour. Their trunks and stripped rear seats could hold 14 cases of 'shine. Their rear leaf springs were suspended over the top of the rear axle which was very favorable for weight distribution and a very low center-of-gravity. Loaded with 'shine, the car hugged the road like a cat on the run.

If a revenuer was right on a moonshine runner's tail in a chase, the runner could do a "big turnaround" in the Ford by throwing it into a sideways skid and tapping the brakes. At just the right reduced speed, he'd yank the wheel around and the Ford would instantly spin about precariously avoiding rolling over. Now, facing in the opposite direction, the runner would cram the stick shift into first gear, slam the gas pedal to the floor and with screeching tires head straight at his pursuer and run him off the road.

I never forgot how close Crafton, Gray and I came to being planted in north Georgia those many years ago. Over the years, I read everything I came across about moonshining. It turned out to be excellent background for my novel, "Moonshine Express. "

Rod Norville

History of Moonshine Today and Yesterday

Moonshine began in the foggy glens of northern Ireland and Scotland where whiskey originated. These northerners from the British Isles were so persecuted by the English they fled to America. The first ship to leave Ulster, Scotland, was The Friends Goodwill which sailed for Boston in April, 1717.

Over the following decades, the Scottish-Irish fanned out into the backwoods of Pennsylvania, Virginia and the Carolinas where they set up their whiskey-making stills. Whiskey was an integral part of their lives. They considered it to be a health drink (in Gaelic "whiskey" means "water of life"). They mixed it with various herbs for homemade remedies for numerous ailments including fever, snakebite, pneumonia, rheumatism and food poisoning. They sold it to travelers, trading centers, peddlers, immigrants and even to the army. Whiskey was used as a pick-me-up by both men and women when they were cold, tired or depressed.

By the Revolutionary War, one-third of America's population was Scottish-Irish and, being crafty fighters and crack shots, they contributed greatly to the winning of the war. Of the 56 signatures on the Declaration of Independence, July 4th, 1776, eight were Scottish-Irish. Davy Crockett, Sam Houston and 11 Presidents, including Jackson, Wilson and Nixon trace their ancestry back to Ulster.

With the Revolutionary War won, the Scottish-Irish backwoods patriots returned to their farms and stills. Unfortunately, the war had left our country deeply in debt and George Washington's Secretary of the Treasury, Alexander Hamilton, decided to put an excise tax on all distilled spirits to help reduce the debt. The tax was passed March 3, 1791, and became the first internal revenue statute (IRS) in the country's history.

After much bickering, the Scottish-Irish rebelled against the tax in the Whiskey Rebellion of 1794 but were put down by President Washington's militia from surrounding states. The Scottish-Irish Pennsylvania backwoodsmen decided to move on to Kentucky where soil and climate favored the growing of corn - the key ingredient for their "white lightning" corn whiskey.

The early settlers discovered corn in America and learned how to grow it from the Indians. The Scottish-Irish backwoods ancestors from Pennsylvania had always used rye grain for their whiskey until they tried the corn in Kentucky. They'd found a winner! Corn whiskey was the best.

They came up with a new recipe. They placed corn into a container with holes in the bottom and poured water over it for a few days. Corn kept wet and warm would sprout. After that, they would dry the sprouted corn and grind it into 'corn grits'. Corn grits would be turned into a 'mash' in a container including hot water, sugar and yeast and, in a few days, it would ferment and be ready for the distilling process.

Although distilling whiskey is an art, it simplistically involves heat, vaporization and condensation. The mash is put into a pot (like a big tea kettle with a long spout). The spout is connected to a copper condensing coil called, "the worm". The "tea kettle" is heated to above the boiling temperature of alcohol (176 degrees F) but below the boiling temperature of water (212 degrees F). Alcohol vapors boil-off and, under pressure, leave the water and mash behind and rise into the copper coil. The coil is cooled by circulating water and condenses the alcohol vapor into clear liquid alcohol - hence the name, white lightning.

Red whiskey came about as an accident. A 'shiner, outside of the little community of Bourbon, Kentucky, ran out of good whiskey storage barrels and had to fill a barrel damaged by fire. Some months later, he opened the barrel and found his clear white lightning had changed to a rich amber color. He promptly named his discovery, Bourbon Whiskey.

James C. Crow, a chemist from Scotland, was the first distiller to take the art out of distilling and replace it with science - the use of a thermometer and a hydrometer and stressing cleanliness throughout the process. His whiskey is known as Old Crow.

With the onset of the Civil War, the Federal Government re-imposed excise taxes on whiskey and tobacco to fund the Union army. After the war, the Reconstructionist Government, faced with enormous debt, kept the taxes in place and the Revenue Bureau of the Treasury Department was formed to seek out moonshiners who weren't paying the tax.

In 1871, General George Custer was ordered to march his troops into Kentucky and wipe moonshining off the map. But, the Kentucky backwoodsmen weren't any more intimidated by the General than was Sitting Bull later is his career. The mountaineer Kentuckian was strong, lean with keen ears and had the eye of the hunter. He walked and fought like an Indian and had incredible endurance. (Sergeant York, the most decorated soldier of the First World War, was that kind of backwoodsman). General Custer marched away without accomplishing his mission

By 1877, there were over 3,000 moonshine stills in the Appalachian mountains and moonshine had spread into Mississippi, Arkansas, Alabama, Georgia, Florida and Tennessee. The Appalachian mountains had the three very favorable ingredients for moonshining; corn, water and, because moonshining was illegal, isolation. A moonlit night in a remote spot was the most favorable time to make the booze unobserved and the term, "moonshine", took hold.

Some of the Floridian moonshiners were halfbreed Seminole Indians. When white men poured into Georgia and Alabama in the 18th century, many of the Indians fled to Florida. They were called Seminoles, meaning runaway lovers of freedom. They took up farming in north Florida and welcomed terrified black runaway slaves into their society. This disturbed the Government and it sent General Andrew Jackson, soon to be our seventh president, with his army to defeat the Seminoles, return the runaway slaves to their owners and cart the Seminoles off to a reservation in Oklahoma. The Seminoles sent General Jackson packing.

After our Government attacked the Seminoles again in two more wars over 30 years, it gave up and some of the Seminoles, along with their black friends, faded into the swamps and learned how to distill moonshine whiskey.

The Seminoles were never defeated, never signed a peace treaty and some still live in the swamps of Florida.

Moonshiner's heritage and mind-set throughout the country was not to trust Government oppression of any kind and they withdrew from easy access. They devised ingenious systems of signals and alarms to evade Government intruders. They insisted that a man who decently raised his family and paid his taxes, had a right to grow his own corn and make his own whiskey.

They quite often worked together since it takes at least two people to properly operate a still. By the end of February, they'd cut the wood so the blustery March winds could dry it out and prepare it to cook the whiskey. In April, they'd split the wood. May through August, they'd grow the corn. August through October they'd make their 'shine. After that, they'd bury or hide their stills.

In 1894, Congress raised the whiskey tax to $1.10 per gallon hoping to increase the government take in revenue. But that simply expanded the amount of untaxed moonshine being made. Moonshining was becoming so profitable that honest farmers started making it. The government estimated in 1896 that up to 10 million gallons of bootleg booze per year was being produced. (The term, bootlegger, came from salesmen from the previous century who would fill their high-topped boots with flasks of illegal whiskey and sell it to the Indians).

At the turn of the Century, moonshining was still concentrated in the Blue Ridge mountains, western North and South Carolina, northern Georgia and eastern Tennessee but it was now spreading rapidly into other states. Government revenuers were forced to become hunters experienced in smelling cooking mash and following the streams the moonshiner needed for water to cool and condense their still's alcohol vapor into "mountain dew".

At the same time, Temperance was becoming a major issue. There was a clamor to prohibit the sale of any alcoholic beverage. State "dry laws" were passed in Alabama, Georgia, the Carolinas, and Kentucky. The consequence was that even more farmers started making 'shine.

Leading the Temperance movement was a very imposing woman named Carrie Nation. She stayed in the headlines leading a group of outraged wives and mothers in an attempt to outlaw all alcoholic beverages. As a group, they singled out saloons and chopped them up with hatchets.

Carrie, and her followers, wanted prohibition for the entire country. A noted church publication at the time declared: "All ungodliness comes from intoxicating liquor, and if we destroy it, the whole world will become Christian."

Calmer heads pointed out that no less a revered figure than Abraham Lincoln had gone on record decades earlier saying, "Prohibition will work a great injury to the cause of Temperance."

Nevertheless, Prohibition was established on October, 28, 1919, when the 18th Amendment was passed. With it, the price of moonshine liquor leaped tenfold and a multitude of farmers across the land from Florida to California, from Indiana to Texas, turned to making moonshine. Within weeks after the Amendment was passed, former bar and saloon owners were applying to city and county governments to turn their establishments into soft drink parlors.

Night clubs stopped selling liquor, but found loop-holes to still make money by selling corkage fees to patrons who brought their own white lightning. The clubs also required that patrons buy their expensive set-up drinks like ginger ale and lime rickey soda.

The rich, anticipating the coming prohibition, had filled their cellars with booze to overflowing by 1919. This encouraged "robbin' hoods" who burglarized those homes and took the booze from the rich and sold it to the poor. The newspapers reporting these burglaries were read by a very sympathetic audience favoring the "robbin' hoods".

Prohibition evasion soon was considered a "sophisticated" and "smart" thing to do. A favorite joke of the time had to do with a revenue agent following a man with amber liquid sloshing out of his rear pocket. The agent seized the man and caught a few drops of the liquid in his hand and tasted it. He snarled, "Scotch, huh?" The man answered, "No, Airedale."

The original moonshine states - the Virginias, the Carolinas, Kentucky, Tennessee, Georgia, Alabama, and Arkansas - greatly increased their production. Moonshining in their hills had become "big business" by rich crooks who invested in a chain of moonshine stills throughout the area.

In New York, a man named, McCoy, brought in European booze by ship and parked just outside the three-mile limit from New York. New Yorkers would make their way out to the ship in small motor boats. Wanting to be sure they were getting good booze from McCoy's ship, they'd yell, "Is this the real McCoy?" Thus, the origin of the popular saying.

In Texas's eastern Jefferson County, moonshiners were plentiful. They mainly operated their stills in dense forests or in the marshes where sea grass grew over 12 feet tall. During a summer dry spell in the middle of Prohibition, a fire broke out and, fanned by a high wind, quickly engulfed over eight square miles of thick sea grass. After the fire died down, over a hundred charred stills could be observed by the revenuers along with the bodies of many 'shiners who couldn't outrun the fire.

Washington and Oregon were supplied with booze slipped across the border from British Columbia, Canada. Montana had its own converted ranchers to 'shiners supplying their needs.

A wonderfully documented book on the history of California's bootlegging years, "One Eye Closed and the Other Red", describes how whiskey filled ships from Mexico, the Caribbean and Tahiti parked off the Northern California coast. Some of the whiskey would be sold offshore and the balance unloaded in the middle of the night at Moss Landing near Monterey Bay. The latter would be driven north to the San Francisco bay area with paid-off police clearing the way.

Early during Prohibition, a steamer named Washington boldly came into port in San Francisco with 30 drums stenciled "COFFEE" consigned to the Northland Coffee Company of California. Unfortunately for the steamer, there was no such company and the drums were opened by the authorities. They each contained 50 gallons of whiskey that were confiscated.

Northern California also had its share of home-grown moonshiners mainly in the wine country but also ranging all the way from the Pacific Ocean to Lake Tahoe. An old-timer from Mendocino County remembers, "We'd run off a batch. We didn't really know what we'd made, so we'd take a gallon or so and go 'round the country and give everybody some. If nobody died, we knew it was good enough to drink."

In Southern California, illegal booze poured across the border from Tijuana, Mexico, just as drugs are pouring across today. Southern

California itself had its own roaring moonshine business, mainly in the desert, and contracted for by Los Angeles gangsters. One of the federal agents at the time became so frustrated about the deserts of Riverside and San Bernardino counties, he said, "If the desert gets any wetter, Noah will have to build another ark."

Another old-timer recalled, "Our still was in the Mojave desert near a reservoir. After we'd get through distilling the 'shine, we'd dump the used-up mash into the reservoir for the ducks to eat. Figured we was destroyin' the evidence. Them ducks would get so drunk they couldn't even fly."

A Boron, California historian, Donna Fairchild, reported another incident involving a drunken animal: A chap named Murphy worked for several Los Angeles syndicates and made Turtle Juice (the term Turtle Juice implied it was made from cactus but it wasn't; just corn as usual).

One evening, a single employee was on the night shift in Murphy's camouflaged still when a bull wandered by. The bull was munching on desert grass as he moseyed onto a little sandy knoll. The knoll, however, was a man-made cover hiding Murphy's still. It had a corrugated tin roof covered by sand and a few planted desert shrubs. The bull crashed through the camouflaged roof and landed square into a huge 9,000 gallon vat of fermenting mash.

The employee was able to get a rope around the bull's horns and save his life, but by morning the bull was dead drunk when Murphy and the rest of the crew arrived. They were able to get the snockered bull out of the vat with a crane but not before he'd deposited a big pile of bull dung in the mash. The foreman asked Murphy, "What shall I do with this batch?" Murphy casually answered, "Run it. A little bull dung never hurt nobody."

There was even a thriving moonshine business on Catalina Island, "22 miles across the sea" from Southern California. Agents had a big bust on Marille Street and poured a huge amount of 'shine into the street. As it continued fermenting, it smelled like vinegar. Very old-timers still call Marille street, Vinegar Hill.

In Scottsdale, Arizona, cowboys started making 'shine. On the Internet, an old-timer tells the story of a cowboy 'shiner who established his still in the middle of the desert more than 30 miles outside of Scottsdale. His trail followed dry desert washes across the Fort McDowell Indian Reservation and the Verde River. One moonlit night, he loaded his truck with 'shine to make a delivery to Scottsdale. When he arrived at the Verde River, he chose a place to cross where the river spread out and was only knee deep.

As he slowly drove across, he heard galloping horses approaching, Indian's war whooping and guns being fired. The Reservation Indians knew about his whiskey and were intent upon having some. The cowboy grabbed his revolver and, keeping his truck between himself and the approaching Indians, floated down the river for several hundred yards. He hid in the brush listening to the Indians yelling and shooting as they tore into his whiskey. They stayed and drank the night away.

By daylight, the Indians were all passed out and the cowboy slipped back into his truck and quickly drove what was left of his load on into Scottsdale.

By 1921, it cost $3.50 to make four gallons of 'shine that sold to the end user in the cities for $162.00. A customer could buy the 'shine at "speakeasies" all around the country. Speakeasies were unmarked places where alcohol could be purchased. A patron who was trusted, would be given directions to the speakeasy. When he found the place, he'd knock at a door. A guard on the inside would open a tiny window and ask for a password before the patron and his date could enter and partake of the "giggle juice" inside.

To make the moonshine go further, look and taste better, it was cut with water, glycerine, food coloring, and extracts. The addition of cheap wood alcohol and embalming fluid killed dozens of drinkers and blinded and crippled many more. Junk car radiators full of lead solder were used as condensers. This resulted in lead poisoning. An unethical 'shiner named Jake served up a batch of poisoned 'shine that crippled everyone who drank it. Their limps were so distinctive they became known as having "Jake's Leg".

Greed even reached into the backhills and caused some good hill's 'shiners, who prided themselves on their "mountain dew", to start delivering the "heads" and "tails" of a still's run. Both of these runs are poisonous. The first run-off (heads) is weak, impure and full of water and rank oils. The last run-off (tails) will be nearly 200 proof (100 percent alcohol), and too strong.

A book from the era titled, "Homemade Wine and Beer: A Neatly Compiled and Arranged Collection of Formula", became very popular with its recipes to make white lightning taste and look like conventional booze. The following samples from the book allowed bootleggers and bathtub gin makers to take white lightning and convert it into the following popular drinks:

Scotch Whiskey

Neutral spirits, four gallons; solution of starch, one gallon; creosote, five drops; cochineal tincture, four wine glasses full; burnt sugar coloring, quarter of a pint.

Gin

Neutral spirits, five gallons; water, five gallons; add glycerin and oil of Juniper.

Jamaica Rum

Neutral spirits, four gallons; Jamaica rum, one gallon, sulfuric acid, half an ounce; acetic ether, four ounces; burnt sugar coloring, eight ounces.

Another story in "One Eye Closed and the Other Red", tells of a bootlegger in San Francisco who sold a thirsty pool player a pint of white mule (another popular California name for white lightning). The pool player complained, "Hey, I wanted brown stuff, not this fresh alcohol."

The bootlegger answered, "This is the same stuff, just clear-not brown."

The pool player said, "Oh, no. This is moonshine. I want the real stuff."

"Alright, I'll be right back with the kind you want."

In a few minutes the bootlegger returned, "How's this nice brown whiskey?"

"Yes, that's what I want." The pool player said and took a big swig and reentered the pool hall.

The bootlegger smiled and spit some more tobacco juice onto the sidewalk.

The prohibition of the twenties attracted the worst of the criminal element and it affected the entire population. Every schoolboy knew the names of the big-time hoodlums such as Al Capone and Dutch Schultz who had their competitors "rubbed out", either shot, like in "The St.Valentine's Day Massacre", or tossed into the ocean with their feet encased in concrete.

The criminals of the era brazenly built their own distilleries, terrified police, witnesses and judges and murdered Federal agents. The huge growth of crime shocked millions of once Temperance-minded people into the unwilling conclusion that the worst saloons were better than this.

The criminals control lasted for 14 years but was severely curtailed over time by Elliot Ness and his "untouchables". Prohibition finally ended in 1933 when the 21st Amendment to the Constitution repealed it.

Family fortunes still exist today, such as the Kennedy family of Boston, that were founded on the larceny of their fathers or grandfathers in the '20s.

The Commission of Internal Revenue only had about 3,000 agents to police the entire country during prohibition. But underpaid as they were, they had impressive records. In 1920 alone just 18 of them destroyed 1,000 stills and made 1,000 arrests.

After Prohibition, moonshining slowed in some parts of the country but never stopped. It continued right on and still exists in areas of the Carolinas, the Virginias, Kentucky, Tennessee, and Georgia and to a lesser extent in many other states.

For example, in 1961, in Dawsonville, Georgia, the community's most generous citizen contributed to every charitable cause. Unfortunately, he was also Georgia's biggest moonshiner. Every ATF (Alcohol, Tobacco and Firearms) agent knew the generous citizen but found he was too well-connected to be caught.

They tried unsuccessfully to infiltrate his organization with wiretapping. Finally, in 1962, things went their way. They inspected an enormous chicken house that covered a huge still with a 20 foot diameter boiler and 54 fermenters holding over 200 gallons each. There were also 1,260 gallons of moonshine and 10 tons of sugar. Unfortunately, none of the recovered evidence could be tied to the generous citizen so the agents blew the whole place up with dynamite. (I've wondered if the generous citizen may have been the boss of the runners who spared Crafton, Gray and myself a few years earlier).

In the late '90s, The Savannah Morning News reported: "Moonshine is fading from coastal Georgia. It started in the '70s, when the price of sugar went up and caused moonshining to go down. Moonshining is still there but marijuana is now a bigger problem. Between July, 1995 and July, 1996, 18 stills were busted along the coast, but only three the following year." An agent commented, "Moonshiners are just getting old."

In 2000 however, the Associated Press reported: "In the foothills of North Carolina two men work quietly in a narrow, tin-roofed shed at the end of a rutted road winding behind a chicken house. Hoses snake along the broken concrete floor, and tiny flies attracted by the sweet aroma of ground apples swarm by the thousands. Cobwebs hang from dusty rafters. 50 pound bags of Dixie Crystals sugar line the walls, and a rusty Frigidaire is stocked with two-pound bags of Fleischmann's yeast.

Along one wall stretches a row of huge vats, big enough to bathe in, fashioned by hand from white pine. Each vat holds a concoction of 300 gallons of spring water, 300 pounds of sugar, 50 pounds of rye and a pound of yeast. It is frothfully fermenting.

John, a heavy man in bib overalls with gray stubble on his face, a wad of tobacco in his mouth and a John Deere cap on his head, says, 'The mash for this sugar liquor needs to bubble for another day or two before it's ready to go into the cooker.' He pauses. 'There ain't many people left who knows how to do this,' he adds and wipes his brow."

A dying breed?

While John may consider himself part of a dying breed, the Federal Government says moonshiners in the South are alive and doing very well. The agents are waging a modern war on white lightning with wiretaps, night-vision goggles, surveillance cameras and electronic tracking devices.

A retired supervisor with the North Carolina Alcohol Law Enforcement Division said, "It ain't like Snuffy Smith when he had the little copper kettle behind his house and made some for himself and his neighbors to drink."

The moonshine industry has evolved from an illegal folk art into a big business involving dozens of suppliers, distillers and distribution from Roanoke, Virginia to Johnston County, North Carolina. Today's mega-moonshiners use huge stainless steel stills that take up entire barns and produce hundreds of gallons of 'shine per day.

A retired revenuer maintains, "There's 50,000 gallons of untaxed liquor leaving southwest Virginia alone every year."

Special Agent in Charge, Jeff Roehm, of the Bureau of Alcohol Tobacco and Firearms (ATF) in Washington D.C. told my reporter that "Operation Lightning Strike', started in August of 1988. It involved a number of families in a country store in Virginia. So far, there have been 31 convictions in the case. Authorities seized over 2 million dollars in profits from the operation. The modern moonshine was transported in heavier-weight plastic jugs similar to the jugs used for milk distribution.

This bust didn't kill moonshining in the southeastern United States though. There were still plenty of backwoods stills throughout the South as well as high-tech large operations organized like modern businesses. The larger operations sometimes deal in marijuana as well. The author was recently in east Texas and was told there are still moonshine busts every year of old 'shiners and the clientele hasn't changed much. The 'shine is still sold at a dollar or two per shot.

Special Agent Roehm also told my reporter, " We've tracked illegal liquor from West Palm Beach, Florida all the way to New Jersey. The thrust of the manufacturing appears to be centered in North Carolina and Virginia."

Roehm continued, "There is a huge profit motive in making moonshine even today. The bootlegger can keep literally all of the profits and not have to pay state or federal taxes. There are "nip' Joints in Washington D.C. and along the East Coast in Philadelphia and Baltimore, where moonshine is sold under the counter. Millions of dollars in state and federal tax revenues are lost each year due to moonshining."

Roehm also explained that more ATF agents lost their lives during prohibition than any other time in history. They were shot or crashed their cars during high speed chases of bootleggers.

Supervisor Bart McEntyre, Resident Agent with ATF in Virginia told my reporter that on the black market, moonshine is often half the price of liquor in the stores. A lot of state and federal taxes are involved in the sale of alcohol. Basically federal taxes are $13.50 per gallon. Each state also has their own taxes.

McEntyre went on to say, "I know in the last eight months, in Philadelphia, there was a large illegal still seized. Also, authorities have recently followed illegal liquor trafficking to Texas and Florida."

In Virginia on October 23, 2002, police were investigating a routine disturbance complaint when they noticed a chemical odor often associated with a methametamine lab. They arrested and cuffed the owner. As they were hauling him off, the owner said," Hey, buddy if you don't mind, would you go into my bedroom and turn off the propane gas." The police found cooking moonshine in the bedroom!

Jenelle Johnson, also with ATF in Washington D.C. told my reporter, "A moonshiner can be charged not only with not paying taxes, but also for violating the federal statute against making illegal liquor."

Alcohol and Beverage Control Investigator, Mike Hauser in Yuba City, California, told my reporter he was involved in the arrest of one person during the seizure of an illegal liquor still in Sierra County in Northern California during December, 2002. Hauser said that the size of the still indicated the suspect was using it to produce distilled spirits for the purpose of selling them. The seizure was carried out after an area bartender offered an undercover officer a sample of the illegal liquor. Hauser pointed out that the production of beer and wine is legal in the U.S., but that within the state of California even a dismantled whiskey still is considered illegal and constitutes a felony.

Equally as important as the moonshiner is the "runner" or "bootlegger" who transports the illegal whiskey from the hidden stills to hundreds of markets. Folks like I met in the '50s. They transport the 'shine on country roads in the middle of the night in "souped-up" cars traveling well over 100 miles per hour.

A typical night in the life of a bootlegger would involve driving one of three souped-up cars: a '40s Ford in the '50s and a '50s Dodge or Chrysler in the '60s. One of the cars held the whiskey. A second car was loaded with five gallon cans of high-test fuel. The souped-up cars burned a lot of fuel going well in excess of 100 miles per hour on their run. This second car was to supply additional fuel to the whiskey car during the run. The whiskey car didn't want to be stopping at local gas stations. A third empty car was to start the transfer by making a dry run looking for ATF agents. The driver of the empty car would make the entire run of 20 miles or so at full throttle hoping to draw out any hidden ATF agents hidden along the side of the road. He would then slowly backtrack using a spotlight to look for hidden agents' cars in the woods.

If the coast seemed to be clear, the empty car would make the run again at full throttle with the whiskey car, also at full throttle, a mile behind. If an ATF agent suddenly appeared, the empty car would try to entice the agent to chase his empty car. The third car with the spare fuel brought up the rear. His purpose was to top off the other two car's gas tanks if required and, if the whiskey car driver had to ditch his whiskey-loaded car, he'd pick him up.

Thomas R. Allison's MOONSHINE MEMORIES includes the memories of a retired ATF agent: "I would back my car into the woods and cover it with a couple of brown blankets. I'd take a broom and sweep the grass I'd backed over to eliminate my tracks. Then I would hear it. The distant sound I was waiting for; a whining of tires of a vehicle traveling at high speed and the roar of a powerful engine as it sucked in vast quantities of air through two four-barrel carburetors. The adrenalin would flow. I liked to be hidden fairly close to a railroad track crossing because at high speeds an unloaded car would leave the pavement for a moment or two while flying over the slightly elevated railroad tracks. I'd hear a distinctive break in the whine of its tires. From that sound change, I knew it was an empty car trying to draw me out. I'd watch it sail past and wait. A few minutes later, I'd hear another high speed car coming. If there was no momentary sound change when it crossed the tracks, I knew I had my whiskey car and I'd give chase. That's when the fun really got started on Thunder Road!" (Robert Mitchum starred as a bootleg runner in a movie named, Thunder Road).

As bootlegging boomed, the drivers started racing among themselves to see who had the fastest car. Those races evolved into stock car racing in the late '40s and from there into modern day NASCAR racing (The National Association for Stock Car Auto Racing). A beloved early bootlegger/stock car racer was Bill Elliot known as "Awesome Bill from Dawsonville." NASCAR affectionados will also remember NASCAR legends and bootleggers, Junior Johnson and Lloyd Seay. Seay won the Lakewood 100 in Atlanta and the next day lay dead from a single gunshot to the head from an argument over moonshine sugar.

Fast cars and fancy driving weren't the only way 'shine was transported. A couple of my Air Force buddies in the '50s, Lightfoot and Bishop, were recruited by moonshiners to smuggle 'shine into Savannah, Chatum County, Georgia. Bishop owned the car, Lightfoot was the "talker". Chatum County was dry at the time, but South Carolina, a few miles away, was wet.

The 'shiners offered Lightfoot and Bishop $30.00 each plus an all expense paid weekend once per month. All they had to do to earn the $60.00 was to dress in their Air Force uniforms and drive to a designated motel in South Carolina and check-in on a Friday evening. Lightfoot would tell the desk clerk, "We're having car trouble and have called a mechanic that can repair it this evening. We're gonna walk on down to the diner and get a bite. Here are our car keys. Please give them to the mechanic who'll be by shortly to pick up the car."

At check-out in the morning, another clerk would hand them back their keys and a sealed envelop from the "mechanic". Once in their car, they'd find it loaded with 'shine to just below window level. They'd open the envelop and find directions to a motel they were to stay in on Saturday night outside of Savannah.

At check-in at this motel, Lightfoot would repeat his car trouble story and leave the car keys with the clerk. In the morning, the day clerk would hand them back their keys with a sealed envelop from the "mechanic". Back in their now empty car, they'd open the envelope containing $60.00. Thirty dollars each was a lot of money to them. They only made about $120.00 a month at the time. And, they'd had very little risk because revenuers didn't suspect 18-year-old Airmen of bootlegging.

Bootleggers are even more sophisticated today relying on subterfuge. Following is an article in the San Jose, California Mercury News on February 16, 2003 and written by Carol Emert:

"WINERIES IN STATE RESORT TO BOOTLEGGING"

"Wine Country has a dirty little secret.
Bootlegging - the stock-in-trade of whiskey-peddling mafiosi in the 1920s - is common practice among California wineries in these modern times.

While prohibition ended 70 years ago, the 1930s-era laws in 37 states still restrict wineries ability to send vino to customer's homes. Those restrictions have given rise to a stealthy network of Wine Country shippers who use tricks such as repackaging wine bottles and labeling them as olive oil to move them across state borders... ."

Moonshining and bootlegging aren't going to go away as long as there is a buck to be made by circumventing the law and, of course, there's a kind of historical and romantic lore to it all as well. The South loves moonshine history just as I do. For example, New Prospect, South Carolina, hosts a Moonshiner's Reunion every October and Dawsonville, Georgia-Georgia's moonshine capitol-holds a Moonshine Festival every year.

So that's the history of moonshining without going into minutia. I've tried to identify and acknowledge all the information sources I've gleaned from the people interviewed, books and the Internet.

You probably noticed the history included the time and place of my following novel, Moonshine Express. Enjoy!

Rod Norville

CHAPTER 1
Rob Tells His Story:

Me and Katie stole a train the summer we both turned thirteen. We didn't have no choice; it was a life or death sort'a thing. It all began one pretty usual mornin' when I came up from a deep sleep, banged my palm several times in the vicinity of the alarm clock and successfully disarmed this daily enemy. I reviewed my interrupted dream and recognized it as one of those recurrin' kinds, mom and me diggin' for turtle eggs while she explained there'd been a mistake. She hadn't died at all! She'd just gone over to a Tallahassee clinic where her cancer had been miraculously cured. She was home again. I sat up and swept a damn cowlick outta my eyes. I rolled out of bed and disturbed Epidus curled up on the comforter. Ep' raised her homely head, gave me a dog smile, and wagged her German Shepherd tail. I scratched her ears before shufflin' into the bathroom to clean up.

Carefully examinin' my face in the stained mirror, I worked with a surgeon's skill over the array of blackheads that had bloomed recently after the Townsend cake I downed on my birthday. I dabbed each operation with a wash cloth before proceedin' to the next eruption and worked steadily until my face shone back at me, beamin' an image of jaunty healthy glow. After brushin' my teeth, I soaked the damn cowlick and plastered it to my skull. Peerin' in the mirror with my best Elvis Presley pout, one I'd seen him use recently in one of his old movies on television. Satisfied I was a handsome devil, I moseyed over to the bedroom closet where I rummaged around for my cleanest "dirty clothes".

Epidus flopped off the bed, prepared to help in any way she could. We went into our little kitchen. I poured a bowl of Alpo for Epidus, and Wheaties for myself. The Formica dining table was cluttered from dad's "party" durin' the night, so I fed myself standin' over the wood cookin' stove.

Dad's raspy snorin' came through the curtain coverin' the entry into his larger bedroom as I packed a lunchmeat and mayo sandwich and an apple into a brown paper bag. I dreaded my final chore of the mornin' gettin' dad up and movin' toward his job in the Newton soft drink bottlin' plant. The pitch and duration of his snorin' told me that he'd tied one on a little worse than usual last night. I pushed the curtain aside and slowly entered his room. It was even shabbier than the rest of our little tin-roofed shack that looked like it was 'bout to fall in the river and smelled permanently of dirty socks and Old Grand Dad.

"Dad! Wake up and get a move on. You're gonna be late." My father flung an arm out in protest. "Dad, you can't be late again. You know what your boss told you. Please, dad ... please ... wake up." I pulled on his arm. The two pleases made it through and my father popped open his eyes. "It's okay, boy, I'm awake." His breath was enough to make an alligator puke.

"I'm going to pole the flat-bottom out to my fish line after school, dad. Maybe bring home a catfish for dinner."

He rolled out and promptly grabbed his forehead in both palms and moaned. I looked on in sympathy and hazarded, "Dad, maybe you're drinkin' a bit much of late." I was enterin' dangerous territory.

It was the first time I'd tried it since mother died. I'd practiced it several times in bed while dad was skindivin' in his whiskey glass at the kitchen table drinkin' and smokin' and after awhile carryin' on a one-way conversation with mom. I dreaded goin' through the kitchen to the bathroom durin' the night 'cause of his mood changes. At dinner, he was my father of old, interested in my school and friends. In the mornin', he was crabby, sick and real tough to get up. But, the worst time was in the middle of the night when he'd be real unnatural like happy and would pressure me to listen to a slurred one way conversation. From time to time, he'd laugh to hisself.

Last night, I'd tried to slip past him after takin' a whiz but he seen me and I got stuck for half an hour listenin' to his gibberish before he pushed his bottle away, stood, weaved and mumbled, "Time for bed."

This mornin', he glared at me and lurched toward the bathroom as if he was goin' to puke. A blast of alcohol covered me and I held my breath. I figured I'd pushed far 'nough for a start and grabbed my books and scooted out.

"Don't worry about dinner, dad." I yelled back through the door, "I'll fry up the catfish and make hushpuppies like mom used to. See ya tonight." Epidus just missed gettin' her tail caught by the slammin' screen door.

It was a two-mile walk into the little village of Newton along a red clay lane borderin' the river. Newton was named after old Bill Newton who'd built a local paper mill that the village grew around. My pa worked in the mill right up to when it fell on hard times a couple of years back when Bill Newton's grandson, Harold Newton, converted it to a Dr. Pepper bottlin' plant servin' the area all the way up to Tallahassee. He was able to keep most of his employees, like my pa, on the job. The Doctor-that's what most everybody calls him, is also the only sawbones in town.

3

Our closest neighbor, Eloise Brown, was already sittin' long the riverbank next to her shack. The early mornin' sun gleamed on the shack's unpainted cypress walls, weathered grey and smooth.

"Mornin', Ms. Eloise. What'cha fixin' to catch?"

"Mornin', Rob. Hopin' for a nice Roe Shad." She was ageless in appearance, small, stooped and wiry with a sweet face like melted chocolate. "How's your pappy this mornin'?"

I grimaced. "Up and about." I wondered why she was askin'. I hoped she didn't know about my dad's recent descent into the bottle. Eloise looked out onto the river and saw her cork dip and then settle back.

"I wish he'd let me muck out your old house. It's missin' your momma's lovin' care." She started to pull her fishin' line in hand over hand. I shook my head. "I do the cleanin'. Dad don't accept handouts."

"I'd like to do it just to pays my respects to your fine momma. I loved her near as much as you did." Eloise inspected an empty hook and reached into a rusted coffee can full of black mud and worms. "It's too much for a boy your age to do school'n and take over your momma's chores as well."

She selected a fat wiggly worm and baited her hook. "My young'uns are all raised, I got nothin better to do."

I shifted my weight from one foot to the other. "I can't talk for my dad, and besides, we're doing just fine. 'Preciate the concern, Ms. Eloise."

"The Lord giveth and he taketh away, Robby. I shore don't understand sometimes how he chooses those he takes. Your momma was fine folk."

I hated it when Eloise would start her primitive Baptist malarkey. "I got to get to hustlin' or I'll be late for school."

I pointed at my dog. "Leave Ep' here with you?"

Eloise shook her re-baited line back into a quiet, darkly shadowed part of the river close to shore. "Why I'd be flattered to have your company, Miss Epidus." She patted a grassy place

4

beside her.

Eloise knows a lot of stuff and ever since I was small she liked to pass it on to me. At about the time dad got me Ep' as a pup, Eloise told me an old Greek story about a guy named Oedipus Rex who killed his father and married his mother-is that gross or what-but I liked his name. I was pretty young myself at the time and have never been sure if it was Eloise or me that screwed up the Oedipus into Epidus. It don't really matter. Ep' and me both like it the way it is.

"Mrs. Appleby don't like her hangin' 'round the school all day." I explained. I stroked Epidus' head, ordered, "Stay," and moseyed on. The path veered away from the river for a spell through a grove of live oaks, palms, and Spanish moss-covered pines. A mile down the path, I passed Milton's General Store, a palmetto log structure where the river people purchased there staples. A quarter mile further, the path tucked up close to the river again. That's when I heard the drone of an airplane.

Lookin' up, I couldn't see nothin' what with a grove of old pecan trees 'tween me and the river. The drone sounded closer and closer. It sure sounded like it was comin' down just beyond the grove so I bolted like a jackrabbit through the trees, my heart thumpin' like an Indian drum; I knew there was no place out there a plane could land. I broke through the trees and skidded to a stop. A two-engine plane with big pontoons under each wing settled into the misty fog hangin' over the water, bounced a couple of times and then coasted out of sight behind a bunch of moss-covered pines toward shore a hundred or so yards further on.

I remembered there was an old wooden fishin' dock up there nobody much used no more so I got back in gear and made tracks for it. Just before I cleared the trees a voice I knew brought me up short.

"Where in hell 'ave you been?" Joe Crafton yelled as soon as the plane's propeller quit flappin'. I moved behind a tree. I'd recently had enough trouble with Mr. Crafton to last me a spell.

The pilot stepped out of what looked like an army surplus amphibian supply plane painted camouflage style in dirty brown and green. He dropped onto one of the pontoons and caught a rope that Mr. Crafton tossed him from the dock. The pilot was a skinny white man in khakis and so short it looked like he'd been sawed off at the pockets.

"Sorry, Joe, but that crazy cuss was with Dooley again and wanted to know our business arrangements. I came as soon as I could break away." His voice was damaged by years of smokin'.

Mr. Crafton pulled the plane up tight against the dock and tied it down. "You shouldn't have come at all when you saw it was gonna be light when you got here," he grumbled. "You know the rules."

"Tell ya the truth, Joe. I'm too scared of that guy not to let him talk."

Mr. Crafton shook his head in disgust. "Lets get to unloadin' before it gets any later."

Mr. Crafton backed his dark blue Ford pickup to the end of the dock and they proceeded fillin' it with large cardboard boxes with pictures of Chiquita bananas on some, Sunkist oranges on others and peaches and other fruits on the rest. They was heavy 'cause Mr. Crafton had to strain lifting them into his truck.

I found it prudent to quietly back off into the trees and head on to school. I wondered what they was up to but decided this was one time I was gonna mind my own business.

Back on the path, I saw the Newton mansion through the wispy mornin' fog. It was a two story, green-shuttered Victorian set on a lush green grass covered hill. The roof was covered in hand-hewn cypress shingles. Slip grown geraniums and fuchsias covered a surroundin' porch and wide screen veranda.

Katie Newton hugged her mother goodbye inside the veranda and then skipped out to the road. "Morning Robby."

"Mornin', Katie. You sure look super this mornin'. Like a blond-haired angel come down to bless us less fortunate."

Katie's rosebud mouth scowled. "Your baloney is as welcome as an outhouse breeze, Robby McKinley."

I grinned. It always struck my funny bone when she talked like Eloise. It was so out of character what with her breedin' and all. "You should'a seen what I just seen," I said. So much for mindin' my own business.

"What's that?" Katie asked. "An old army seaplane just landed out in the river and unloaded boxes of fruit into Mr. Crafton's pickup."

"Sounds like Mr. Crafton's brother-in-law, Rusty Yates from Smithtown. Daddy sometimes calls him to fly really sick patients to the hospital in Tallahassee." She headed on down the path.

"But, Mr. Crafton's your daddy's manager at the plant," I said when I caught up with her. "Why'd he be meetin' this plane?"

Katie smiled. "Daddy doesn't mind if his employees get other part-time jobs. I've heard him tell mama he encourages it." She shook her head at me. "He's worried about keeping every-one on at the plant. I've overheard him tell mom how he's in-structed Mr. Crafton to come up with plans to beef up produc-tion and tighten up expenses."

I said, "Mr. Crafton was boilin' that the plane was late landin' after daylight," I protested. "What'cha think about that?"

"Probably wants to deliver the fruit while it's still nice and fresh. He'd also want to be done with the delivery and be at the plant as quick as he could."

I chewed the inside of my check for a moment. "Reckon you're right. You finish the math problems?"

Katie's head spun around and her eyes mirrored a kind of bright blue innocence. "Of course, Robby. Didn't you?"

"Got a might busy."

Her smile faded. "You'll be copying my homework again?"

"If you don't mind."

Katie made a cluckin' sound with her teeth. "It's getting to be a habit since your mother passed ... I'll let you one more time, but you're never going to be an airline pilot at this rate."

We stopped under the magnolia tree across the path in front of her house. I took out a clean lined piece of paper from Katie's three hole notebook and proceeded to copy her results in large bold pencil strokes. Katie's fine penmanship had contained all three problems and their solutions on just one side of her paper. My copy rambled over both sides and was scrunched up toward the end.

"Thank ya kindly." I smiled and threw my head back with a flourish to dislodge the damn cowlick coverin' my left eye. "Anythin' I can do in return?" Katie carefully reinserted her homework paper into her notebook. "Front tire is low again on my bike."

"Well. I'll patch it after school. Stick the tire in the river and find the leak. I'll teach you how to patch it yourself, if you'd like. I know how you hate to depend upon others to do your stuff."

Katie gave me a half smile. "Well, in the last year you've taught me how to bait a hook, set a crab trap and shoot your little .410. If daddy knew I was out in the marsh shooting a shotgun, he'd have a spit fit."

I grinned again. "I be takin' my boat out this evening to my catfish line." I carelessly folded the paper and stuffed it into my shirt pocket. "Wanna see it?"

"Your boat? When did you get a boat?"

"Ms. Eloise gave me her son John's. She says he's got a dandy job in the cotton gin over in Clancy and a girlfriend he's fixin' to marry. Says he won't be needin' his boat no more."

Katie gathered up her books and lunch pail. "What kind

8

of boat is it?"

"An old flat -bottom, big enough for two people. Needs bailin' from time to time, but it gets me out to the deep quiet water where John set his catfish lines."

"He taught you how?"

"Yeah, I'll teach you too, if you wanna come."

Katie frowned, looked down at her polished Oxfords and didn't answer. I looked at her with a puzzled expression. "What's wrong?"

"Nothing"

We walked on in uncomfortable silence and then stepped off the tire- tracked hardened lane into the grass as we heard a car approachin' from our rear. Dr. Newton's black Buick slowed and pulled to a stop beside us. The driver's window rolled down.

"Good mornin', Dr. Newton," I greeted.

He was a heavyset man with long thinnin' hair combed horizontally to cover a bald spot. As usual, he was wearin' a gray suit with a green bow tie. He nodded politely toward me.

"Katie, don't forget what we talked about last night."

Katie looked down at her feet and swung her lunch bucket in front of her.

"Well?" Dr. Newton asked.

"I won't, daddy," She whispered while studyin' her shoes.

"And come straight home from school."

Katie nodded, severely embarrassed, and her father rolled the window back up and pulled away in a puff of dust. I can't say I much cared for Dr. Newton. I figure him for being so henpecked he molts twice a year. I asked Katie, "What was that all about?"

She looked down for a bit and then appeared resigned to 'fess somethin' up.

"Daddy thinks we're seeing too much of each other."

"Whoa, take that back to the startin' line an' run 'er through again, slow."

"He thinks I'm becoming too much of a tomboy. Wants

9

me to spend more time with my girlfriends doing more 'lady like' stuff."

I took in a huge gulp of air and kind'a sounded like a quackin' goose lettin' it out. "You mean he don't want you spendin' your time with the son of a Florida Cracker." I was afraid this was comin' 'cause of recent events but I was still wounded to the core. I realized my face was all squashed up and it made me think of Mrs. Juliason, my fourth grade teacher, who'd spent most of that year bawlin' me out for one thing or another.

Katie looked up. "That's not fair Robby. My dad isn't like that. After all, you so-called 'Crackers' are all either Scottish or Irish ... just like we are."

My heart felt like a threshin' machine.

"Don't you believe me? You've got the same brown hair as my dad, just a lot more of it."

I was too angry to risk sayin' any more and stalked off like a Storm Trooper causin' Katie to have to skip to keep up.

"Are you sulking? Can't we have a mature conversation?" Katie trotted along side. "I feel as bad as you do about daddy's orders, but I know he's doing what he thinks is best ... Robby aren't you going to say anything?"

I picked up the pace.

"If you're not going to say anything, you can just walk to school by yourself!" She waited to see what I was going to do.

"Go ahead," I blurted out like a damn fool. "You don't need to be seen with the lower class." Mother had always told me it's better to keep your mouth shut and seem a fool, than to open it and remove all doubt.

Katie's eyes was now as icy blue as a year old ice cube in the freezer part of our old fridge. She stopped in her tracks and put both fists on her hips, her lunch pail in one fist and a brown canvas sack with her school books in the other. The silence was as brittle as glass. I was just sick, but wasn't about to let on. I'd let the worse possible thing happen. I'd argued with the girl I loved.

Stormin' on like an idiot, I entered the old single room school house with off -white stucco walls and asbestos shingled roof. I was early, even Mrs. Appleby hadn't arrived. But I didn't want to wait outside for the bell to ring and have to face Katie again. Slumped down in my seat, I stretched my skinny legs into the aisle.

"Move your feet."

I looked up and saw Joe Crafton's son, Billy, glarin' down at me. 'Here we go again,' I thought. Billy had been givin' me a rough time ever since his pa told my dad and Dr. Newton I was a sneak thief and he'd ordered me to stay off'a his property. Billy was the pitcher on our softball team, and the most popular boy in class. He'd lined up most of the boys in the class to help in makin' my life miserable. I couldn't stand him.

I slowly drug my feet toward my desk. Billy impatiently kicked them aside and started to stroll past. His face, long and narrow like his dad's, glared down at me.

"I wouldn't be doin' that again." My voice dripped venom kind'a like my dad's does when he's pissed.

Billy turned and put his hands on his hips. "Well butter my butt and call me a biscuit, what'll you be doin' if'n I do?"

"That's for me to know and you to find out."

"Pretty tough, huh?"

"Tough enough."

"I could rap you up side your snot box quicker'n you can get out of that seat."

"I wouldn't try."

"If I don't, it just means I don't want to get my hands dirty."

I raised out of my seat and looked up at Billy. He was half a head taller'n me. "Whatta ya mean?" I said.

"That you're a grime is what I mean. You wear the same clothes to school every day. They're probably giving you a melvin by now and you can't get 'em off."

"Take that back." Shovin' on my desk, I stepped out

11

into the aisle.

"Screw you if I will."

The other students was enterin' around us and lined the aisles on both sides. One of the girls started gigglin'.

Billy's best friend, Pete Francisco stepped up. I wouldn't call him overweight, maybe just a foot too short. He whispered to Billy, "Here comes Mrs. Appleby. Tell grungy you'll kick his ass after class."

"I'll kick your ass after class."

"I'll be there." I kind'a grunted. Personally, I figured in a fight with Billy I was going to last about as long as a grasshopper in a chicken yard. Sittin' back in my seat, I saw outta the corner of my eye that Katie was standin' by her desk across the aisle listenin' to the whole damn thing. I was mortified that she'd heard what Billy'd called me.

Mrs. Appleby came through the front door and strutted up the side aisle with her big boobs stuck out and her arms and shoulders swingin' like she was carryin' a drum in a marchin' band. She was dressed this day in a too big flowered dress she probably hoped would make her look skinny. The class quieted down and scooted into their seats. Billy turned toward the front of the class, folded his hands and sat up straight.

Mrs. Appleby called the class to order in her Sherman Tank- rollin' through town voice. "Was everybody able to do the problems? " She looked around over the top of wire-rimmed spectacles shoved far down her nose and noticed my agitated state.

"Robby, how about you?"

 Wavin' the dog-eared paper I pulled out of my pocket, I mumbled, "Yes ma'am, no problem for me."

Mrs. Appleby nodded real nice like and questioned several others. She then asked Katie to copy her work on the blackboard.

As soon as Mrs. Appleby's back was turned to the class, Billy turned around and mouthed, "I'm gonna knock you plumb into next week!"

Pete Francisco was seated immediately behind me and leaned forward to whisper some bad breath in my ear, "You're going to be buzzard bait after class."

It was a long, long mornin'. Billy Crafton was the strongest kid in class; tall and wiry built like his dad, all sharp edges and angles. He pitched a softball like a pro with a full 360 degree vertical windup, not the wimpy little figure 8 horizontal windup of all the other guys in class who tried to pitch. What made it worse, Billy and his pa had Sunday supper regularly with the Newtons. I was paranoid that Katie admired Billy. If a fight started, I'd have to do well or be humiliated forever.

Well, dad taught me last summer how to hold my hands and stand in a fight, catch blows on my elbows and duck my head instead of jumpin' back the way I wanted to. Always, always get in the first punch. Dad said most fights will stop right there.

Mrs. Appleby's voice droned on with about as much warmth as an icicle, but I was fixated on what I'd have to do if there was a fight. Just thinkin' 'bout it made me hyperventilate. My head felt like it was floatin' and I wiped sweat off my upper lip with the back of my hand. I dang near molted outta my skin when the bell rang.

"So, you're a real tough guy, grime," Billy taunted, lookin' down through a shock of wavy, sandy-colored hair.

We'd immediately gone behind the classroom. I sensed that most of the class was circlin' about.

"Kiss my ass," I replied. My voice sounded like a croakin' frog.

"It looks too much like your face," Billy retorted.

"That's the beauty of it."

"There's no beauty in a horse's ass."

With Billy's final one-up-man-ship, I swung a damn haymaker that missed by a foot. Billy jumped back with an astonished look on a face gone white, and then swung his own haymaker. I ducked under it, as dad had taught me, stepped forward and drove a straight left fist into Billy's nose.

We stood toe-to-toe and the crowd started to cheer. Billy had the reach, but lacked my trainin' and took more blows than he gave, swingin' wild, no blockin' incomin' punches. I was winnin' - big time.

I didn't see Pete Francisco step into the inner circle behind me until he suddenly threw his arms around my waist and hurled me to the ground. He jumped onto my stomach and Billy squatted beside me and slammed his fist into my eye.

Epidus started barkin' and I saw her through blurred vision racin' between the legs of my classmates and breakin' into the circle. Ep' saw what Billy was doin' to me and let loose a guttural growl and leaped at him. It all seemed to be happenin' in slow motion. Billy screamed like a hungry baby as Ep' bit down hard on his wrist and drug him off me.

Pete and I flopped over and over in a cloud of red clay dust trying to hit each other. Pete's elbow caught me square on the nose just as Mrs. Appleby arrived and threw her arms about.

"Break this up this minute!"

I landed one more painful one on Pete's ear and a geyser of spit shot out of his mouth. He took off like a scorpion had crawled down his neck. Mrs. Appleby grabbed the back of my shirt and pulled me away. Epidus released Billy's bruised and bleedin' wrist, dropped onto her haunches and moved slowly toward the teacher, growlin' low with bared teeth. Mrs. Appleby let go of me and screamed, "Get that dog away from me!"

"No, Ep'!" I yelled.

Epidus stopped in her tracks and looked at me.

"Get that animal out of here!" Mrs. Appleby hollered and grabbed up the hem of her dress and backed toward the classroom.

Jumpin' to my feet, I grabbed Epidus' collar.

Billy looked at his bleedin' wrist and started to cry like he was hornet stung. "Robby started it, Mrs. Appleby."

Mrs. Appleby's face was red and puffed up like she'd

rolled in some poison ivy. "Get off this school ground, Rob McKinley." She forced her voice to sound real calm like but it still sounded   like a Sherman Tank grindin' to a halt. "You're never going to set foot in my class again."

My nose was bleedin' like an open tap and I wiped my free forearm across it smearin' blood on my shirtsleeve.
I tugged on Epidus' collar and backed out of the yard.
Katie broke from the rest of the class and ran after me.

"Katie Newton, you get back here," Mrs. Appleby screeched.   Katie ignored her and caught up with me.

"I'm going to call your father," The Sherman Tank bellowed.   She was so crabby she couldn't get the acid out'a her system.

Katie looked up at me and said, "I'm afraid you're in deep shit this time, Robby." She looked down at Epidus trottin' along side and added, "Ep' too."

Epidus looked up at us when she heard her name and wagged her tail. She was askin', "Did I do well?"

I patted her head. "We didn't start it. Hot snot kicked me."

Katie brightened. "I was proud of you. I worried all morning that Billy would hurt you, he's so much bigger. You made mince meat out of him."

I did an 'ah shucks' kind'a shrug and said, "You better get back to school. I don't want you in no trouble on my account."

Katie shook her head. "Not until we stop your nose from bleeding."

I agreed. "Reckon it's best to give Mrs. Appleby a little time to calm down."

Katie said, "She looked kind'a funny backin' away from Epidus with her dress pulled up like that."

I grinned. "She's got calves only a cow could love."

We both cracked up a bit with nervous laughter and I calmed down a tad. "It was sure swell, you standin' up for me like you did." Wipin' my nose again on my sleeve, I added, "And I'm real sorry I was such a dimwit on the way to school."

Katie smiled up at me. "And I'm sorry Billy called you a grime. You know, he's turned into quite the snot since his mother took off with another man last summer."

Grittin' my teeth in embarrassment, I stuttered, "Reckon I didn't know I looked so bad."

"Robby, you're practically raising yourself. You have nothing to be ashamed of." She inspected my bloody sleeve. "My dad has talked to mom about how things must be for you."

"What does he say?"

Katie paused and looked at me real careful like. "Promise you won't get mad again?"

"Promise."

"He says your dad has been drinking way too much ever since your mother died and he's concerned how it's affecting his job and you."

My shoulders did a little nervous tick dance of their own as I threw my head back to get the cowlick out of my eye. "My pa gets to work on time and we're doing just fine. And that's a fact!"

"I told you last month, Mr. Crafton told daddy he'd caught you prowling around his place late at night. He was sure you were trying to steal something. Daddy said with your father's heavy drinking, you're not getting proper supervision." Katie looked at me close. "Tell me honest-to-God, you weren't trying to steal anything, were you? You never did tell me what you were up to that night."

"No, of course not." I could feel a flush climb right up my neck and spread across my face. "After pa went to bed that night, I noticed Ep was out'a Alpo. So, I grabbed some change outta the kitchen grocery money jar and me and Ep' made tracks for Milton's before it closed."

"Milton's doesn't close until ten," Katie commented.

I nodded. "I got the Alpo just as they was closin'. I got

to worryin' pa might wake up and find me gone, so, me and Ep' cut through Mr. Crafton's field as a short cut home. Well, you know that barn of his?"

"That old building down by the river?"

"Yeah, that's it. Well, in passin', I thought I saw a light leakin' out'a crack in the sidin' so I took a look through the crack. Just then Ep' started barkin' and next thing I knowed, Mr. Crafton grabbed me by the ear and spun me around."

"What did he say?"

"He called me names that wouldn't improve Sunday school none, kicked me in the butt, and told me to get the hell outta there and to not come back."

"Did you?" Katie asked.

I looked away. "When my pa got home from work the next evenin', he told me Mr. Crafton told him he'd caught me sneaking around his house lookin' for somethin' to steal."

"That barn is no where near his house."

"I know. I tried to tell my dad what I'd seen, but he was mad enough at me to kick a hog barefoot and wasn't into listenin'."

"What had you seen?"

I shook my head. "What looked like a conveyer belt and crates of uncapped bottles. Like a small bottlin' assembly line."

Katie stopped and put her hands on her hips. "You didn't answer my question about staying away from the barn. You did go back, I bet, if I know you."

"I was real curious if Mr. Crafton was goin' into compe-tition with your dad," I laughed nervously, "so 'bout the same time of night a week later, I went for a better look. But this time, I didn't take Ep', just a flashlight."

"What did you see?"

"It was dark and quiet as a cemetery. I flashed the light through the crack and took a good look around, but all I could see was a bunch of empty cardboard boxes lyin' around on the other side of the wall."

"So, you jumped to the wrong conclusion the first time."

"Umm. I don't know, maybe," I answered.

"I'm sorry about what my dad did this morning." Katie reached out and almost patted my arm. "Sometimes he wakes up cranky 'cause he's worried about the employees. Goodness knows, he checks in with his plant manager every morning before he goes into his office. Then he works terrible hours. You know, he's the only doctor between here and Tallahassee. He sees every pecan farmer, rancher -just everybody. Even the people who live deep in the swamp come to him when they need doctoring."

I interrupted. "Your daddy just wants to break us up."

"That's not true."

"Oh no?" I side stepped an arm's length away. "Well he's been out to see my pa twice in the last month."

"Because of Mr. Crafton?"

The first time, yeah, but not the second. After the second time durin' supper, pa looked down into his plate and asked me why I don't spend more time with my buddies."

Katie skipped to keep up. "What did you say?"

"I said you was my buddy."

Katie smiled and ran a hand through her hair. "And?"

"Pa looked up at me and said, 'You know, boy, you and that gal ain't exactly members in the same country club."

We turned up the Newton mansion lane lined with a white picket fence. Katie said, "That's not right, Robby."

I said, "I'm sorry. I shouldn't of said nothin'. I got my motor mouth goin' before my head was in gear."

We entered the mansion's veranda. Epidus stopped at the steps and looked up at me.

"Stay!" I ordered.

"Mother, are you home?" Katie called out. The house was empty.

"Come with me." Katie took me by the hand and led me into the master bathroom. She went through the medicine cabinet and found cotton balls to put in my nose and iodine and a

18

large Band-Aid for my skinned elbow. She pulled my arm over the sink and rinsed the blood out of my shirtsleeve. "Robby, you're the finest person I know and the strongest."

I couldn't stop the smile that spread across my face like a pebble's ripple landin' in a quiet pool. She rang out the sleeve and rolled it up my arm. "Daddy told mother that Preacher Hatchet said he'd tried to get you to talk about your mom's passing, but you turned him off real abruptly ... you've never talked to me about it either."

My eyes scrunched up. I didn't relish talkin' about my mom-ever. It made me 'bout as happy as a woodpecker in a petrified forest.

Katie's blue eyes flashed. "No, I want to say this. You're my best friend and if I'm yours, well you should talk to me about it. You can't keep it bottled up." She studied my skinned elbow.

"I reckon I don't wanna," I growled

Katie frowned and shoved the iodine's glass prong applicator a little harder than I thought was necessary, applied the bandage and unrolled my sleeve.

"Thank you, Nurse Newton."

She soaked a wash cloth and wiped off my nose without a word more. My face reflected back at me from the mirror wasn't lookin' too bad except one eye was startin' to puff up a little. Fidgetin', I said, "You better get back to class and tell Mrs. Appleby you're sorry you run off with me."

Katie nodded. "I'm glad it's Friday. Mrs. Appleby will have the weekend to calm down."

We walked back out onto the veranda and Katie asked, "How's your dad going to take this? You know you'll have to tell him."

"Super ticked off. I sure hope I find a catfish on my line. I'll wait to tell him after supper." I gave her my 'I'm real confident' smile. "He's gettin' to like my cookin'. A nice meal might cool down the big scene I'm expectin'."

Cougar Mountain Junior High School
5108 260th Street East
Graham, WA 98338

Katie opened the front door and stepped outside. "Cooking? Where did you learn? Your mother?"

"Ms. Eloise."

"Like what?"

"Like fryin' fish and frog legs, simmerin' fish chowder, squirrel, crabs ...just about anything." I bragged.

"I hope it works. Robby, I'm really scared for you and Ep'. Your dad's going to have to call Mrs. Appleby."

"I know." I walked over to her Schwinn. "Let me take your bike. I'll patch the tube this weekend and bring it back to school on Monday ... if Mrs. Appleby will let me back in class." I wheeled the bike down the drive and nervously chewed the inside of my cheek thinkin' about facing dad at dinner.

My thoughts was cut short by a train whistle. It was the weekly visit by the short freight that delivered goods to Newton and picked up crates of bottled soft drinks from the Newton plant. I dropped Katie's bike behind the magnolia tree and hustled my buns a quarter mile down to the little freight yard. The engineer had already shut down the diesel electric locomotive to idle and gone inside a little tin shed that served as the freight yard's office.

I slowed to a walk and paced the locomotive's length sniffin' in its smells of diesel fuel, oil and hot brakes; like a prehistoric monster catchin' its breath after chasin' its dinner. I grabbed the hot metal side rails and pulled myself up the steel staircase. The engineer and me had an unspoken agreement I could climb up and look into the cab but not go in. I looked in awe at all the controls and glass covered gages wonderin' what they all did. I knowed when he cranked the diesel back up it would hiss and roar just like that monster bein' jerked awake.

"Howdy, Rob."

"Oh, hi, Mr. Thornly." I answered the engineer.

He swung up into the cabin and waved shipping papers at me. "Better hop down for a minute. I've got to back this over to the dock."

I said, "Thanks for lettin' me look in. I'd better make tracks for home."

CHAPTER TWO
Eloise Tells Her Story:

I see'd Robby comin' down the path pushin' a shiny girl's bike wid Epidus bringin' up the rear. I was standin' in my yard such as it is, spoiled with sand-spurs that'll leap right on your socks if you even walks near 'em.

"Hi, Ms. Eloise." Robby waved

"There's that wily dawg." I shook my finger at Epidus and then took a closer look at young Robby. "What happened to your eye, boy?"

He told me.

I sighed, "Oh, Robby." I bit my lower lip and went on. "That's bad stuff, 'pecially Ep' bitin' that boy."

"What do ya think I should do? It wasn't Ep's fault."

Rob looked 'bout to cry he was so concerned for that ol' hound. Couldn' blame him none. She's real special. My wrinkled up ol' face wrinkled up a bunch more. "Jes tell it to your pappy straight. He won't let no one hurt old Ep'. I jes' hope he can get you back inta school."

My head rocked back'n forth a few times. "I'm sorry, but Ep' done snuck off as soon as my back was turned."

"That's okay, Eloise."

I rested a hand on the shiny chrome handlebars of the bike he was pushin'.

"What'cha doin' wid this fancy girl's bike?"

"Going to patch a flat for Katie Newton over the week-end."

"You sweet on Miss Katie, Robby?"

He blushed from ear to ear. "Reckon that's somethin' for me to know and you to find out,"

"You aim to jes keep it to yourself." I cackled like a foolish ol' barnyard hen and then caught myself. "Maybe that's somethin'to keep to yourself, Robby. Miss Katie is aimin' pretty high for the likes of us river folks as poor as lizard-eatin' cats." "Florida 'Crackers' you mean?"

"Crackers ain't a bad name, Rob. Mean's you comes from farmers that like to eat cracked corn, that's all. Lord knows you could be called a lot worse."

He grimaced and I knew he knew the word I was talkin' 'bout. "On second thought, Robby, I spoke out'a turn. Miss Katie seems a nice young lady ... and nobody's too good for you, Robby McKinley."

"Her dad thinks so."

My brow was startin' to sweat. "Reckon there's a heap o' folks in these parts has the arrogance of the elite. Dr. Newton may be one of 'em." Reachin' down the front of my dress, I pulled out a well worn hanky and wiped down my brow. "Not a bad feller, jes misinformed about who the real elite in these parts are."

Early afternoon storm clouds started rollin' in over the river.

"Let me tell you, it's not the likes of you or me neither. It's the Indians that was here long before any of us."

"Dad told me there's still Seminoles back in the deep swamp." Rob pointed beyond the river. "I'm goin' to pole John's old flat-bottom back in there one day and meet some of 'em."

I felt a shudder right down to my toes. I said, "You got time to jaw a spell?" I nodded toward two weather worn wooden rocking chairs by my front door.

"You wanna give me another dose of Eloise wisdom?" Robby grinned and looked up at the afternoon sun. "Sure. Dad won't be home for a bunch of hours."

He laid the bike down and pulled up a chair. "You gonna tell me about the Seminoles?"

"I'm gonna tell you jes how damn dangerous it is back in thet swamp and why's I don' ever want you goin' in there!" I was nervous as a cat in a room full of rockin' chairs so I got to chewin' my lower lip to calm me down and went on in a nicer voice, "Yes, I'll tell you 'bout the Seminoles ... but they wasn't alone in there by a long shot." I set down and took to rocking'. "There was and is Timucuanes, Apalaches and Creeks as well." I picked up my ol' palm leaf and fanned my brow. "We mostly think Seminole cause they's the Indians my slave ancestors run off to join. In fact, the name Seminole means runaways."

Robby spun his chair around and straddled it. "Eloise, I think you know more history than Mrs. Appleby."

"Lawd, Lawd, you think old Eloise jes' knows 'bout fishin' and cookin'?" Glarin', I leaned forward and stared him straight in the eye. "There's mean folks livin' back in thet swamp. Meaner'n you'all have ever met. Don't you never take John's boat beyond this river." I was so upset I shook my index finger in front of his nose.

"Who are they?" Robby took a swipe at a flock of mosquitoes that had suddenly moved over from the river and was taking delight in bitin' hidden places. "Mrs. Appleby told us about soldiers comin' down from the north a long time ago to control the Seminoles."

I leaned back and rocked. "They tried, but they couldn't

control 'em. Not with Seminole chiefs like Osceola, Coacoches and Alligator. Nobody could beat the likes of 'em."

Robby slapped his arms. "So the Seminoles was the elite in these parts back then?"

"Still are, Robby. They faded back into the swamp out there'n interbred with my slave ancestors." I waved my arm at the river and swamp beyond. "Most of 'em are good people and are the elite " I paused and squinted down my eyes to throw a good scare into him. "But a few are meaner'n stepped on rattle-snakes." I stopped rockin'. "They's the ones I'm warnin' ya about." And I kept starin' at him 'til he was obliged to turn his head.

"They makes their money cookin' moonshine whiskey," I said it knowin' my voice was quiverin' a little. "They shoot or cut up anybody that wanders onto their damn stills."

Robby wasn't real impressed. I considered somethin' for a minute. "I'll tell you, Robby ... but nobody else knows 'cept your daddy ... . " I shuddered. "My dead ... worthless ... mean ... sonuvabitch of a husband was one of 'em 'til he come 'cross somebody meaner'n him that cut his gizzard out." I was so agitated I had to stop talkin' so I started rockin' and chewin' on that lip. I lowered my voice a couple of decibels, "He was so damned lazy he was never caught on the blister end of a shovel, hell, even molasses wouldn't run down his leg; but when it came to fightin', he was willin' to take on a cottonmouth and give him first bite. But goin' up against this 'shiner, he had 'bout as much chance as a worm wigglin' 'cross an anthill."

Robby cleared his throat. "I get your message, Ms. Eloise, and there won't be another person hearin' from me what you just told me."

My face relaxed a little from the scrunched up frown that had frozen it. "I know. You're like your daddy, a feller to be trusted."

Rob swung his leg over the chair and stood up. "I better get a move on and see if I caught any catfish today. I want to tell dad the bad news on a full stomach."

"Good luck to you, boy."

CHAPTER 3
Rob's Story Continued:

An hour after I'd got Ms. Eloise' lecture, me and Ep' poled the flat-bottom out into the Aucilla River and on into a channel filled with water hyacinths passin' slowly by with lifted spikes of bell-shaped flowers. I arrived in the still water and found not one, but two catfish on my line. I poled my boat back under the overhangin' bank through dense and stiff sedge anxious to get supper underway.

"Good evenin', boy." My father, as tall as a burly black oak, slammed through the screen porch door and deposited his lunch box next to the kitchen hand pump. "How was your day?"

I was busy at the wood stove. I'd boned and filleted the catfish, rolled them in corn meal and salt and dropped them into a fryin' pan filled with sizzlin' fat. "Okay," I mumbled, and cupped my hand over my bruised eye like I was deep in thought.

"Somethin' smells wonderful. Are those catfish I see in there?" Dad leaned over and peered into the pan as I scooped

27

them out, golden brown and crisp.

"Yes sir, now for the hushpuppies." I picked up a stack of little cakes I'd prepared from a mixture of fine white cornmeal, salt, a little bakin' powder and egg and dropped them into the smokin' deep fat the fish had just exited.

"Yum!" Dad exclaimed with a handsome grin, "I wouldn't trade your hushpuppies for honest to God cafe cookin'."

The hushpuppies quickly turned the color of winter oak leaves and I lifted them out. "Let's eat 'em while they're hot."

We ate with no conversation and dad never looked up until his plate was clean. I slipped a couple of hushpuppies under the table to Epidus. Dad finally pushed away, wiped his mouth and lit up a Chesterfield. He looked as happy as a fly on a lemon meringue pie until he spotted my eye.

"What happened to your eye, boy?"

I flinched, coughed, and told it all straight like Ms. Eloise had advised. When I finished, dad took a deep drag and his eyes and nostrils dilated.

"So the boss's son done called you a grime 'cause of the way you was dressed?"

I nodded.

"Your fight was two on one?"

I nodded again.

"And Ep' done bit the boy ... did the boy bleed?"

Another nod.

After an ever widenin' silence, dad whispered, "Damn." And took another slow drag on his cigarette. "I ain't mad at ya for standin' up to the boss's boy ... and I'm sorry to the bone 'bout your clothes. I guess I just haven't noticed. But this thing with Ep' bitin' that boy and goin' after Ms Appleby, is bad ... real bad."

He pushed away from the table and stood up. "I'll talk to your teacher tomorrow, but you can't never let somethin' like this thing with Ep' happen again."

He walked outside and stood overlookin' the river.

After a time, he lit another cigarette. He proceeded to get drunker'n a hoot owl durin' the evening and finally staggered off to bed.

Once he was snorin' fit to shake the ticks outta his blanket, I decided I just had'a check out that old barn one more time what with the airplane and all. I figured I only got caught last time 'cause Ep' had barked, so I left her in the house and lit out. Twenty minutes later, I eased up to the barn real careful like. I looked up and noticed a small window I hadn't seen before that was covered from the inside with a black shade. The place was as quiet as a tree fulla owls but a narrow beam of light was streaming through the crack again. I just got one eye up to the crack when a hand stinkin' of cigarettes slammed over my mouth and another arm wrapped around my body.

CHAPTER 4
Dr. Newton Tells His Story:

"Where are you off to, Daddy?" Katie skipped out to the Buick as I was about to back out of the garage.

I spun my head around. The kid must be a mind reader.

It was Saturday morning and I'd slept poorly trying to decide what I should do today. Friday afternoon, I'd had an ear full from Mrs. Appleby about Robby McKinley's fight in school and Katie running off after him. I'd talked in strong terms to Katie at Friday night dinner. Then, Joe Crafton called at damn near midnight and told me he'd caught Robby trying to break into his place again. He was mad enough to kill the boy and I ordered him to send Robby home; that I'd take care of everything. Toward morning, I made my decision.

"Got some business to attend to, hon."

I released the clutch and pulled away before Katie could charm me into telling her what my actions were going to be. Hell, I'd asked Ed McKinley nice enough half a dozen times to discourage his boy from hanging around my Katie. It just doesn't look right, what with Ed working as a forklift driver in one of the lowest paying jobs in my plant. Just last Saturday, I drove out to his place and put my foot down square. I told him in no uncertain terms it'd been okay for my girl and his boy being playmates when they were small. But they're in their teens now and I wasn't waiting for any teenage romance to bloom. Ed didn't take it very well but he couldn't say I hadn't made him a fair offer; an all expense paid military school for his boy. After last night, I'm not taking no again as an acceptable answer.

I pulled up in front of Ed McKinley's house in a cloud of dust and saw my daughter's bicycle on the bank. Robby was dipping its tire into the river. When he saw me, he dropped the tire on the grass and scooted into the house.

I turned off the engine. Ed McKinley swung open the screen door and hitched up his blue overall straps onto his broad shoulders while standing in the open doorway.

"Dr. Newton, honored to have you visit." His voice was as deep as a kettledrum. "Come on in the house."

"Robby," I looked at the boy as I climbed the rickety steps. "I'd like to talk to your father privately."

"Yes sir." He scooted away with his dog at his heels.

Ed offered me a cup of coffee, sat us down at the kitchen table, and politely waited for me to state the purpose of my visit. I choked down a little of the reheated coffee, it was thick enough to eat with a fork, wiped my mouth with the back of my hand, and told him Joe had caught Robby trying to break in again.

"I don't believe it." Ed's voice cracked and he cleared his throat.

"Damn it, Ed, listen close to me." I leaned forward and squinted my eyes way down. "Joe was all for calling the sheriff and having your boy hauled off to the Boy's Farm. It was all I could do to talk him out of it. I told him you and I would come up with a better solution."

"Not the military school," Ed said.

31

"It won't hurt him. I've been trying to tell you for weeks that things are not working out for him or you. I'm talking about one of the finest military schools in the south."

Ed squeezed his callused hands together. "The boy's had it tough enough since my Betty passed over. He'd feel he was bein' punished if I sent him off. I'm all he's got ... hell, he's all I've got."

"Ed, look at it practically. Mrs. Appleby said his grades have plummeted this year. He's inattentive in class, disruptive, disrespectful ... and it all has happened since Betty died, God bless her soul. And, frankly, you're not helping the situation."

"Whatta ya mean?"

"Damn it Ed, do I have to spell it out for you?" My voice went up an octave. "It's your drinking, man. How else could your boy go gallivanting all over the county at night getting into mischief. What I'm offering you will make a different boy out of Robby and give you the time to get past the worst of your grieving and start pulling yourself together."

"I didn't realize I was so obvious." Ed sat with his legs together, his head down. "But sendin' my boy off to military school ain't required."

"You don't understand what I'm offering, Ed. It's my old alma mater and my father's before me. Fort Pulaski Academy in Savannah is a shrine to southern masculinity. You won't know Robby in a year. He'll be trained in the finest cadre in the South, be honed, and have his rough spots polished. When you see him next he'll be glossy and shiny with absolute devotion to the Academy, his country, and you."

"He's already devoted to me." Ed folded his arms and stared up gravely at me.

"Ed," I half raised out of my seat, sloshed coffee onto the table, and pointed my index finger at him. "As president of the school board, I'm telling you Robby cannot continue going to the Newton school. He's a constant disruption to the class and now he's beating up on the other boys and burglarizing your

32

neighbors. He's dragging my daughter down with him and I won't have it."

I could see a red flush start climbing right up his neck and start to fill his face. I could feel the anger suddenly surround him like heat from a potbelly cast iron wood stove, so I sat back down and calmed my talk. I probably sounded like a radio advertisement for the academy; molding feckless boys into leaders, boarding school for the most pedigreed families in the south, a sentinel of responsibility and a bastion of antiquity.

"Ed, if Katie had been a boy, that's where I'd have her right now. It's not going to cost you a thing."

"I understand your good intentions." Ed interrupted.

"Hell Ed," I angled back in my chair and hooked my thumbs in my pockets. "I intend to send Katie to an elite girl's high school up in Atlanta and then on to Smith College. I want her to become a southern lady of breeding. I can't have her swearing and acting like a damn field hand. I'm offering you, at my expense, a chance to do the same for your boy. Change his whole outlook on life, give him some manly virtues and old values."

"I don' know, Dr. Newton. I'll think on it."

I stood up and waved the now empty coffee cup at him. "The time for thinking is past. The Fort Pulaski plebe system builds men, prepares them for the hardships of life. He'll establish friendships and comraderies that will stay with him and help him through life. You've got to take me up on this. For Robby's best interests and yours."

Ed reached into his shirt pocket, shook a Chesterfield out of it's pack and toyed with it. Despair reflected out of shiny eyes when he finally looked up at me and slowly shook his head.

I walked to the door, opened it and the looked back at him. "You've got no choice, Ed." I lowered my voice. "Not if you're going to go on working for me."

I stepped outside and saw that Robby and his dog had moved from the river closer to the house and were watching us.

Robby had a hand on his dog's collar. One of his eyes was covered by a sweep of hair. I walked the few feet to my car and turned back to Ed standing in the open doorway. I knew there was one more thing I had to say and it caused a sudden gas pain just beneath my sternum. "And Ed, that dog is going to have to stay tied ... or be put down. The community can't have a dog on the loose that's attacked a youngster for whatever reason."

I felt like a bigoted bully as I drove away, but hell, I couldn't have my daughter marrying a sneak thief too nosey for his own damn good.

CHAPTER 5
Rob's Story Continued:

I'd been workin' up the nerve to tell dad 'bout last night ever since I rolled outta bed this mornin' and checked out my face in the mirror. Now it was too late. Dr. Newton was here to tell dad all about it. Me and Ep' scooted over to the river after dad and Dr. Newton got to talkin' and sat under the old magnolia tree hangin' over the river.

The summer I turned six I learned to swim and dad climbed out on one of the tree's limbs and tied one end of a hemp rope to the limb and let the other end dangle down almost into the water. He then pulled the loose end over to the trunk and tied it. I still spent happy hours durin' the summer swingin' far out like a clock's pendulum and droppin' into the water rolled in a ball to make the biggest splash. Once in the water, I make a big fuss pretendin' to be drownin' and Epidus leaps from shore, swims out and takes my arm in her mouth and pulls me to shore. It's a game we've enjoyed for years.

We now sat quietly, and I absentmindedly skipped the

flattest rocks I could find across the water. Epidus watched me close, waiting to hear me yell, "Run for it, Ep'!" her queue to fetch. She seemed to sense something very serious was in the makin'.

I picked up just enough of Dr. Newton's conversation to get the drift. He sounded so narrow-minded he could probably look through a keyhole with both eyes. My stomach tied itself into a knot. I edged a little closer to the window. I could see the rear of Dr. Newton's ample butt sittin' at the kitchen table. My dad was lookin' at the floor. I eased back to the river. "My goose is cooked, Ep'." I reached down and scratched her ears

After Dr. Newton left, dad just sat at the kitchen table the rest of the day starin' into his coffee cup. I figured he was thinkin' on all the ways he was gonna skin me, but at dinner, he just said real quiet like, "Let's talk a spell, son."

He didn't ask me nothin' 'bout last night, he just started talkin' 'bout what a chance in a lifetime this Fort Pulaski place was gonna be and all Dr. Newton was gonna do for me. I wanted to interrupt and tell him why I'd disobeyed him and gone back to Crafton's barn, but I realized I hadn't really seen nothin' much all three times I'd nosed around. And besides, I didn't have the heart when I saw the misery in my dad's eyes. He told me that just the tellin' was as hard for him as tryin' to scratch his ear with his elbow. I'd heard enough of his conversation with Dr. Newton to know he was in no bargainin' position.

I managed to paste a sort of smile on my face. "Hey dad, I can handle it." I entered my bedroom and closed the door behind Epidus. My shoulders started to shake. I fell onto my lumpy mattress and pulled the comforter over Epidus and me. "I've got to leave you too, Ep'."

She licked the tears off my face.

"And dad's gotta keep you tied." I kissed her shaggy cheek and watched her head droop as she fell asleep in my arms. I laid awake most of the night listenin' to the old refrigerator chuggin' and squeakin' to itself and at one point the sink burped moodily. I was gonna miss this old house.

I spent Sunday on the flat-bottom with Ep' doing 'buddy' kind of stuff. I told her she was the finest dog anywhere and how much I was going to miss her. That night, I stayed awake for several hours strokin' her sleepin' head thinkin' of Savannah, an old city up the coast of Georgia two hundred miles from Newton. I knew from Eloise it had quite a history, what with bein' a penal colony before the Revolutionary War and bein' the last stop on General Sherman's mean-spirited march to the sea durin' the Civil War.

Monday mornin', I put my school books into the Schwinn's bike basket and wheeled it over to Eloise's shack. I found her in the yard splittin' kindlin'. I told her about Dr. Newton's visit.

"Leave'n tomorrow?" She stammered, "How could Dr. Newton arrange gettin' y'all into sech a place so fast?"

"He's an important contributin' alumni, is what I heard him tell dad. Plus, the school year is just startin' and the sooner I'm there, the easier it'll be on me."

"Robby, a feller's gotta do what his pappy says and I knows y'all cain't refuse, but I'm so sorry."

"I can handle it, Eloise. 'Preciate it if you'd keep an eye out that Ep' eats her food and doesn't miss me too much."

I started to choke up so I grunted, "Got to get movin'."

Katie was waitin' behind the magnolia tree across from her house.

She'd been cryin'. I dropped the bike and for the first time ever put my arms around her.

"Daddy told me everything. Why did you go back to the Crafton's?"

"I'm sure he's up to no good," I said.

"Tell me why you think that," Katie sniffled.

"Things wasn't meshin' in my mind. The old barn had been empty long as I remember. Then, all of a sudden like, Mr. Crafton's out there workin' on somethin' in the middle of the night."

Katie interrupted. "But there was nothing going on a week later ... you told me."

I said, "There was last night."

"Daddy's real upset about last night, but he won't talk to me about it." Katie put her hand on my arm. "What happened?"

I sighed, "There was lights in the barn again so I snuck up close for a peek. Just as I was gettin' ready to take a look, that pilot fella grabbed me from behind and called for Crafton. Mr. Crafton came slammin' out lookin' like a red-eyed bull. He knocked me ass-over-a-kettle an' started kickin' me all the time yellin', 'Whadya lookin' for, you nosy little bastard!'

After a time, he said to the pilot, "I gotta make a call"

They led me off to the house and Crafton told the pilot to watch me. I started to say somethin' to the pilot, but he shook his head and said, "I ain't interested, kid."

I could see Crafton talkin' on a phone through a closed kitchen window. He suddenly hung up and came out and told me to get the hell home. I didn't stop to chat none."

Katie asked, "What do you think is going on?"

I said, "My dad told me your pa is too busy doctorin' to pay much attention to what's goin' on at the plant. He leaves everything up to Crafton. Crafton even writes out and signs my dad's paycheck." I postured a bit and continued. "It seems to me, Crafton's in a real good position to run your pa's plant outta business while he's settin' up his own plant in that barn to replace it."

Katie shook her head. "Your imagination is running away. Daddy says Crafton does a good job and he's confident the plant will be in the black just as soon as Crafton expands the distributorship into some of the bigger towns around."

"I don't trust Crafton." I grumbled.

"You just don't like Crafton." Katie corrected. "You're jumping to a pretty outrageous conclusion just because you've seen him working in his own barn a couple of nights."

I knew she had me. "I guess you're right."

Katie suddenly hugged me tight. "You can't go Robby. What am I going to do without you?"

"Come on, Katie. Look at the bright side. When you see me next summer, I'll be polished and honed." I stepped back and held her shoulders. "Hell, chock full of manly virtues."

Katie smiled through her tears. "Robby, I love you."

Waves of ecstasy shot up and down my body. "I love you too, Katie."

"Then kiss me goodbye before somebody comes along and sees us."

I tilted her head up to mine and gave my best kiss ever-actually my only kiss ever.

"I'm sure gonna miss you, Katie."

Katie shivered to my touch. "I'm going to miss you, Robby McKinley. I'll write you every day you're gone."

"I'll write you every day too." I promised my vision of beauty. I smelled her scent like the aroma of dew on newly cut grass. After a good more talkin', I picked up her bike and pushed it forward. She took it as prim as a preacher's wife at a prayer meetin' and I asked her to turn my books in to Mrs. Appleby.

Before I got up the next mornin', I hugged Epidus for several minutes and explained what was gonna to happen.

Dad, Ep' and I found Eloise waitin' for us at the pickup with a homemade Townsend layer cake drippin' with hot sticky icing. I hugged her gruffly and climbed into the pickup. I put the cake, napkins and paper plates in my lap. The day was dark with cloud piled on cloud, arrogant with the colors of rose and gray. Lightnin' flickered ominously across the sky like a frog's tongue.

I looked through the rear window of the pickup as dad pulled away. Eloise's eyes was brimmed in tears and she was holdin' a despondent Epidus by the rope she would now be tied to for the rest of her days.

CHAPTER 6
Marvin Tells His Story:

I was marching my squadron back from class when I saw a rusty yellow pickup pull onto the Academy grounds and stop in front of the First Academy building. A big, ruggedly handsome man with a couple of days of stubble on his cheeks climbed out. He was in his mid-thirties and dressed in farmer's blue overalls. A boy joined him who was his mirror image just younger and smaller. He had dark brown hair in need of a haircut. They entered the building and a couple of minutes later, a cadet burst out the front door and trotted across the commons just as I dismissed the troops.

"Sergeant Ellis, the Major wants you straight away in his office, sir!"

I marched into the building and knocked at the Officer-in-Charge, Major Swagart's door.

"Come in, Sergeant." The Major was standing military erect behind his heavy oak desk and had been addressing the father and son.

The Major said, "Mr. McKinley, Cadet Rob McKinley, I want to introduce you to Sergeant Marvin Ellis. Sergeant Ellis will be your Dorm Prefect and Squad Sergeant, Cadet." The major waved his swagger stick for me to sit down as he continued the academy's introduction speech I've heard so many times.

"Our curriculum is predicated on the belief that certain qualities of mind are of major importance: precise and articulate communication " - the major pontificated. "The ability to compute accurately, a grasp of scientific approaches to problem solving; an understanding of the cultural, social, and political background of Western Civilization."

Mr. McKinley uncrossed his legs. I could tell he was a little overwhelmed by the Major and I wasn't surprised. Major Swagart is a big-boned man with a chiseled face and piercing eyes. He's always tan and trim and the image of vitality. He continued on in a clear self -assured voice. "You will be removed from the natural environment of family and community for an intellectual transformation. Our daily schedule never varies, and although it will sound somewhat rigid, you will soon get used to it: The rising bell rings precisely at 7:00, breakfast at 7:15, 7:55 to 8:10 is work period, 8:20 to 9:55 class, 10:00 to 10:10 chapel, 10:15 to 10:40 recess, 10:45 to 12:00 classes, then 50 minutes for lunch. Any questions so far, cadet?"

Rob McKinley looked like he'd been sucking on a lemon wedge. He was slouched down in his chair like he didn't want to be noticed. He shook his head in answer to the major's question. The Major frowned and cleared his voice. "Classes run continuously from 13:20 military time - 1:20 to you, until 3:15, followed by athletics from 3:30 until 5:20. Dinner 6:15 until 7:15, study 7:15 until lights out at 10:30. Any questions now?"

The Major thrust his face forward toward the father. "How about you, Mr. McKinley?"

41

"I don't believe so." The man's deep southern-accented voice contrasted with the Major's northern nasal twang.

"Then I'll give you the tour of the Fort before you head home."

The Major ushered us out.

"We were just in the First Academy building." The Major continued. "The surrounding red brick buildings are classrooms and barracks for the Companies. Rob will be with the other recruit freshmen in R Company. Four Companies make up a Battalion."

The Major swung his swagger stick about pointing out the different landmarks. "This area between the Georgian buildings is called the Commons." He indicated the wide well-clipped yard. "And, the far field straight ahead is the Playing Field. The garden over to your right is the Provost's Garden and the little building just beyond that is the Infirmary."

A bell rang and cadets flowed out of the barracks in their fatigue uniforms.

"Well, Mr. McKinley," the Major put his hands on his hips, "this is the athletic period and if you think you've seen enough, it's a good time for Sergeant Ellis to get your son outfitted and moved into the R Company barracks."

The father hugged his son briefly and said, "I'll be back to take you home over Christmas, boy." He turned and walked to his pickup without saying another word.

The Major tapped his swagger stick to his forehead in a goodbye salute and turned to me. "Come into my office for a minute." He pointed the stick at the McKinley boy and said, "Wait right there."

Major Swagart closed the door behind me and exploded, "What in hell is going on around here! First the son of a newly rich Cuban wetback and now the son of a drunken Florida Cracker." Beads of sweat had popped out on his flushed face. "Did you get a whiff of last night's booze on that man's breath? Whoa, enough to gag a maggot. What in hell is happening to our standards?"

He dropped heavily into his chair, put both elbows on his desk and leaned forward. "Bunk him with the wetback."

"Cadet Romero?" I asked.

He pursed his lips in an unpleasant smile. "We'll keep the pariahs together. You and I are going to make life for them so unpleasant they'll wish they'd never heard of Fort Pulaski. It's up to the two of us to carve the trash out of here. You know what I mean, Ellis?"

"Yes sir."

The Major nodded at the door. "Then get started, Sergeant... and incidently, we never had this conversation. Understand sergeant?"

"Yes sir."

I walked the McKinley boy to the Commissary where he was sized up and handed three institute T shirts and PT shorts, brogan boots, blue-gray fatigues for every day wear, and a salt and pepper dress uniform complete with gray cotton shirt, black shoes and a black field hat.

"This is the 'Bible' at Fort Pulaski Academy." I placed a small pamphlet on top of the pile of clothing already weighing Rob down. "It contains all the rules and regulations. I suggest you read it through between now and dinner. It's got your I.D. number in front, Cadet McKinley."

He seemed to flinch at the title.

"This is R Company barracks and here's your room."

He looked at a number above the open door. R9 and frowned.

"Your roommate is Cadet Romero. Change into the fatigues immediately and use this box to pack up your civilian clothes. Drop them by the administration office on your way to breakfast in the morning for shipment home. We'll complete your indoctrination at that time. You will join your other freshmen for the afternoon classes."

Rob slouched and looked around the room with a grimace.

This one has an attitude problem, I thought. Well, I'm the guy to fix it.

"Good luck, Cadet McKinley." I did an about face and walked out of the room.

CHAPTER 7

Rob's Story Continued:

It had rained all the way to Savannah. Dad tried a little
small talk, but soon we just watched the scenery passin' by as
dad's old truck turtled along. Mid-afternoon, we entered
Savannah on old Victory Drive and a familiar odor of a paper
factory drifted into the window. Savannah looked like it had
been frozen in time a couple hundred years ago. We passed
through and drove east toward Tybee Island on the Atlantic ocean.
A few miles out of town, we pulled up to the black wrought iron
gates of Fort Pulaski Academy.

Within a few minutes, we met the Officer-in-Charge, a
real stiff guy in a uniform with such creases they'd a cut you if
you rubbed against 'em and Marvin, a year or so older than me
with three stripes on his arm. I knew I wasn't gonna like him
much. He was as homely as a boil on a pig's nose with a fat face
that didn't quite fit with his broad shouldered but skinny body.
Pimples was clearly winnin' the battle for possession of his
face. After a lot of talk that went over my head from the Major,
that's what I was told to call him, the Sergeant got me some

of the prison clothin' I was to wear and dropped me at my cell.
It was as bright an' clean as a new mirror an' I was as outta
place as a cow on the front porch.

I sat down on one of the two bunks covered in a gray
rough wool blanket pulled taut in all directions. After a minute,
I got up and walked around the shiny wood paneled barracks.
At one far end was a sign entitled 'Dayroom'. I looked into a
large and mostly empty room with a folded table and several
stacked foldin' chairs against the wall. There was a drinkin' foun-
tain on the inner wall in the middle of the room. It obviously was
some kind of meetin' room.

At the other end of the barracks was a sign entitled 'Latrine'. I'd never heard the word and entered to find toilets and
showers beyond. An adjacent door opened into a large supply
closet full
of toilet paper, soap, and brown cotton towels.

"What kind'a place is this?" I asked myself.

I re-entered room R-9 and threw myself onto the cot. A
shot of terrible self -pity tore through me, but after a
time, I dozed off.

"Who the hell are you?"

I sprang awake and looked at a spindly boy dark skinned
and freckled. He was thin as a shadow with crew-cut black hair.
He was standin' in the doorway with one hand holdin' a couple
of books and the other holdin' the door knob.

"My name's Rob McKinley." I sat up.

"Well, get the hell off my bunk, McKinley."

"Sorry, I didn't know which was mine. The Sergeant just
dropped me off and said I'd be sharin' R-9 with Cadet Romero."

"Crap, I thought I wasn't going to have to share."

The black haired boy walked in and dropped his books
on one of the two desks.

"I'm Romero. Rudy Romero."

He reached under his mattress for a crushed pack of Cam-
els and matches, postured, and lit up. A sick kitten would'a been

plumb robust beside him. "And, where are you from, McKinley?"

We slowly got acquainted, suspiciously feelin' each other out. Rudy was from Miami. His dad owned fishin' boats.

"The biggest fleet in Florida," he bragged.

I implied my dad had a big job in a Dr. Pepper plant near Tallahassee. I quizzed Rudy about the Academy and found he'd only been there since classes started two weeks ago.

"Hazing during Plebe Week has been hell," Rudy said.

"What's Plebe Week?" I asked.

"We're Recruit Freshmen Plebes, they call us-and defenseless against the Upper Classmen."

Rudy flicked an ash into the palm of his hand.

"You're lucky you missed it."

"Like what did they do?"

Rudy took a deep inhale and blew a stream of blue smoke out his nose. "Like made us do push ups until we dropped. Anyone who gave lip back was subject to being stripped and thrown in the pond. It's a week of, and I quote, 'ritualization of humiliation' for freshmen."

"Reckon nobody better not try strippin' me." I bristled.

"I'd like to see you stop them." Rudy stubbed out his cigarette on the heel of his shoe. "You'd better get out of those civvies and into your fatigues if you want any supper." He stuffed the cigarette butt into a pocket.

At six, the bell rang again and I, now dressed in my new fatigues and cap and feelin' foolish, joined my newly assigned squad.

I was pushed into part of a crooked line in front of the barracks. I noticed similar squads lined up in front of the other barracks.

Sergeant Ellis stood in front of the squad with his legs spread and his hands behind his back; called parade rest, I was to learn later. He suddenly slapped both feet together and his arms to his side and yelled, "'Tention- forward -march!'"
I eased into the rear of the pack and stumbled along to the mess

hall as he yelled, "Hut- two, hut- four, hut -two- three- four; it was callin' cadence I was also to learn later. I was careful to keep myself outta his line of sight.

"This here is Rob McKinley." Rudy introduced me as he set his metal tray of food onto a dinin' table already occupied by two fat plebes twins that looked like matchin' book ends.

"Rob, these prosperous looking gentlemen are the most recent descendants of the rich and famous Oglethorpe family," Rudy continued.

"Saw you this afternoon when you arrived." One of the twins spoke up with a mouth full of food. "Where you from?"

"Florida."

"His dad's got an important job in a Dr. Pepper plant down there, Phil," Rudy explained and then added, "Rob, this here is Phil and Bill. Bill likes to be called Billy."

"Big job, huh." Billy spoke up, also with a mouth full of food. "He sure didn't look like no executive to me. Dressed in overalls and driving that old Ford pickup."

"Give him a break." Rudy interrupted.

"Go climb a tree, spatter face." Billy grinned. "Where'd you get all them freckles, anyway?"

Rudy scrunched his face up at me and rolled his eyes. "I fell asleep against a screen door."

Later, durin' the study period, I tried to ask Rudy more questions about the Academy, but he whispered, "Don't talk to me now or we'll catch hell from the sergeant. We're supposed to be studying."

Rudy was goin' through the motions of studyin' when Sergeant Ellis arrived. "Are you all settled in, Cadet McKinley?" He asked with a face so sour it could of puckered a pig's butt."

"Yep, sure am."

"Yep? Yep? Who in hell do you think you're talking to? I'm your Squad Sergeant, scum. Don't you ever address me as anything but 'sir'. Now get off that bunk and stand at attention when I'm talking."

Now, nobody'd ever talked to me like that. I rolled my eyes and pushed myself off the bunk.

"Scum," the Sergeant ordered, "answer me loud and clear-I'm Cadet Recruit Rob McKinley, Sir!"

"I'm Cadet Recruit Rob McKinley, sir."

I looked at him like he was a cottonmouth moccasin.

Taps sounded and a voice from the hall yelled, "Lights out!"

The Sergeant stared me down without sayin' another word until the lights suddenly dimmed. "You don't seem to like me much, McKinley. You got an attitude problem? We'll start working on it tomorrow." His face was all swoll up like a carbuncle. He did an about face and left the room.

Rudy reached for his cigarettes. "Don't let him get to you. He's been treating me like poison ever since I got here."

My eye caught the grounds light comin' through our window and reflectin' off the cardboard shippin' box Ellis had given me. Inside, I found a plastic bag to be used to put my civilian clothin' into for shipment home. There was also a small roll of tape and a markin' pen.

I've just given up Katie, my dad, Ep', and now this guy's threatenin' me. They're not takin' my clothes as well. I made an instant decision, and tiptoed in stocking feet down to the supply closet and returned with several towels.

"What are you doing?" Rudy whispered.

"I'm gonna ship my clothes home," I answered and stuffed the towels into the box.

"You're going to ship those towels? And what about your jeans and shirt, pray tell?"

I taped up the box, addressed it and turned to Rudy. "You won't squeal on me?"

"Hell no. What do you take me for, a snitch?"

I pushed open the window and picked up my clothes now secured in the tied plastic sack. I looked around the room and picked up a metal waste basket and climbed out the window.

Rudy stood at the window, cigarette in hand, and watched me dig a hole with the can deep within a row of geraniums close to the window. I proceeded to plant my clothes and cover them with dirt and flowers.

"You are a piece of work," Rudy said and field-stripped the Camel out the open window.

After I slid under the covers, I noticed Rudy pullin' a magazine out from under his mattress. In the dim lightin' piercin' the window from the pole lights over the commons, I saw it was a Penthouse. I was impressed. I'd only quickly thumbed through one of them once in Mr. Peabody's drugstore back in Newton when Mr. Peabody was busy with a customer. I'll tell you, it was somethin'!

It was lunch of the next day before I encountered Rudy again in the mess hall.

"Ship your civvies home this morning?" Rudy asked with a grin.

"Sure did. Got the rest of the indoctrination too."

"So you're ready for the 'rite of passage'?"

"Yep, and I now know I'm gonna establish some of my life's goals."

Rudy nodded slightly at me as he lifted a forkful of grits. "Don't look up, Rob, but Sergeant Marvin Ellis is coming this way."

"Recruit Cadet McKinley, Romero." Sergeant Ellis came boundin' over with his face all red like he was gonna jump us both then and there. He stopped and glared down. "No, don't you two misfits bother getting up on my account. I can tell you're both going to need a little extra polishing on your rough spots. I'll be by after 19:00 hours and we'll start some polishing."

We stared into our trays like they was as interestin' as the Penthouse magazine. Ellis walked through the jackrabbit plebes all ready to bolt through tall grass. The afternoon seemed to drag on forever. I toyed with my food through dinner. My plebe companions avoided eye contact with us. Rudy was real cool.

"Just act like you don't give a shit," he said. "Ellis can't beat us if we stick together on this."

"Halt, Cadet!"

Me and Rudy was headin' toward the showers with towels in hand when we heard the command. We stopped in mid stride and turned toward Sergeant Ellis.

"Let's go into the day room and hear what your thoughts are on polishing up your rough spots."

Ellis closed the door to the eager and frightened eyes of the other plebes stickin' their heads out of their rooms.

"On the floor, recruit cadets! Give me twenty pushups."

"We dropped to the floor and began. Rudy only made it to about ten before he started foldin' in the middle lookin' like he was made of butter. Ellis put his boot in the small of Rudy's back. "Straighten out there, boy." He looked as mean as a hungry raccoon.

I couldn't help myself. I pushed myself up onto my hands and knees and said, "Don't do that!"

Ellis put all his weight onto Rudy's back splayin' him into a spread-eagle position. "You fixing to stop me, McKinley?"

I bit my lower lip.

Ellis said, "You don't have the nerve, do you hillbilly."

I could taste salty blood with my tongue.

Ellis added, "We'll just add Romero's twenty to yours. Now get back down there.

"Thirty-two, thirty-three, thirty-four ... this looks too easy for you."

Ellis placed his boot onto the small of my back. I flinched and struggled to do thirty-five as Ellis increased the pressure. Sweat ran down into my eyes. At thirty six I collapsed totally pooped.

"Well, tough guy, pushups don't seem to be your thing." Ellis removed his boot and put both fists on his hips. "We better give ourselves another day to find something you two can do to clean up your act."

Back in our room, Rudy said, "That s.o.b. Why's he picking on us?"

"I don't know," I shook my head in exasperation. I dropped onto my bunk and decided to write my first letter to Katie by the light slicin' through the curtains.

Dear Katie,

I'm here in the French Foreign Legion, just kidding, it's the Fort Pulaski Academy. Our day starts with a trumpet blowing reveille. We jump out of our bunks and put on fatigue uniforms and go brush our teeth. A lot of pushing and shoving because we've only got fifteen minutes before they march us off to breakfast in the mess hall. And, we can't go to breakfast if we haven't made up our bunks with 'hospital corners,' like they do in hospitals, I guess.

It's really all spit and polish all day long. It's not an easy job for them to transform us into robots. It's march here, march there, and constantly being yelled at by everybody who has been here longer than us.

Today we went to the quad and were taught the basics of the manual of arms. My new buddy, Rudy, knew all about it and kept whispering jokes about it in my ear. He talks so much he could keep a windmill going. He's from a rich family, heck all these kids are. The difference with Rudy is he's elite, like Eloise would say.

I miss you and will write you every day. We have mail call after dinner and I sure am anxious to get your first letter, Rob.

The days passed slowly. We had to look forward each evenin' to a new 'hazin' by Sergeant Ellis. On the second night, we had to sprint a hundred laps around the parade grounds. When we returned to R9, we was soaked in sweat and Rudy was as green as a Florida avocado. "You alright?" I asked.

He flopped onto his bunk on his back. "Yeah, how 'bout you?"

I grinned and said, "He's really getting' us into shape."

There was no way, short of Ellis swinging' a machete near my privates, That I was going' to let him get me down.

On the third night, Ellis told us to get into full dress uniform and marched us for an hour around the parade ground. The other plebes watched out their windows-pleased it was us and not them.

I waited every evenin' for mail call and was the only plebe who never got nothin'. My name was finally called the third week and with a shaken' hand I opened the letter. It wasn't from Katie. It was from Eloise:

> *Der Rob,*
>
> *Yor daddy gave me this adres. I sees him from time to time and hes looken good. Don't need you getten him up. Does jes fine by hisself.*
>
> *Epidus misses you and luks for you every day after school, so I's ben taken her for walks in the wetlands every day so she can chase Osprey birds. I sure misses you.*
>
> *Love,*
> *Eloise*

Receivin' Eloise's letter made me awful happy, but apprehensive. I had discounted not gettin' a letter from Katie as being the mail service from little Newton. But, Eloise's letter made it, why not Katie's? Katie's first letter arrived two days later. With a poundin' heart, I took it to my room. Rudy pulled his Penthouse out from under his mattress and took off for the dayroom to give me privacy.

> *Dear Robby,*
>
> *I'm sorry to be so late writing, but I had to wait to get your address from Ms. Eloise. I miss you something terrible and I can hardly wait for school to end so I can run home to see if your letter has arrived. I sure hope I get a letter from you soon.*
>
> *The day you left, I told daddy the only reason you'd gone back to the barn was you were suspicious Mr. Crafton was going into competition with our plant. Daddy asked if you'd seen any-thing to confirm your suspicians. I told him no. Daddy said I*

was to stop defending you; that you had become a sneakthief and that was that. I said you weren't. Daddy then said Mr. Crafton told him you stole a lot of things over the last few months, always at night and after he went to bed. I'm mad as a wet hen at his lies and am going to find a way to prove he's lying.

There's also something else interesting for you to know. Three days after you went to Fort Pulaski, I stopped at Milton's to get a banana when I was out walking Buffy after school. There wasn't any fruit at all except for some stale figs. I asked Mr. Milton where the fresh fruit was that Mr. Crafton had delivered recently and he looked at me like I was crazy. He said whatever fresh fruit he has for sale is grown by locals.

I miss you and can't wait for your first letter.
Love, Katie

CHAPTER 8

The weeks passed in a blur of marchin', schoolin', and Sergeant Ellis just gettin' meaner'n a rattlesnake in a hot skillet. The best part of every day was the quiet time after lights out and my nightly conversations with Rudy. Rudy kept me laughin' with his fun-makin' on the hot-snot staff, and the big headed upper classmen.

"You'd think they was never freshmen themselves from the way they strut around so stuck up they'd drown in a rainstorm. I bet if it was known, their family trees' ain't no more than a bunch of shrubs."

I saw early on that Rudy tired real easy. He told me it was somethin' called a heart murmur and made me promise not to tell no one else. I thought he oughta go see Captain Tuton, he's a doctor in charge of the infirmary. He's also second in command to Major Swagart, but a lot nicer.

I anxiously waited for every mail call and Katie was good to her word, a letter a day, usually with a little P.S. remindin' me she still hadn't got a letter from me. I didn't understand, 'cause I'd written every day.

> *Dear Katie,*
>
> *I don't understand where my letters are going. I must have sent you a couple of dozen by now. They aren't being returned here so the Post Office must have misplaced them. You'll probably get a whole bag of them delivered one day soon.*
>
> *Rob*

> *Dear Robby,*
>
> *It's been over seven weeks and I still haven't received a single letter from you. I'm very tempted to walk out to your dad's to see if he's gotten any letters from you, but my dad would kill me if I did. He won't even let me talk about you at the dinner table. For example, one night at dinner shortly after you left, I tried to tell daddy about you seeing that amphibian plane land on the river and unload fruit boxes into Mr. Crafton's pickup. Daddy just cut me off and told me not to be gossiping about Mr. Crafton. He said the plant was continuing operating at a loss and he didn't know how much longer he could keep the doors open. He said he was pleased Crafton has come up with a part-time job.*
>
> *I'd better leave now for school. I always leave a little early so I can mail my letters at the post office because daddy doesn't want me writing you. Maybe today will be my lucky day and I'll finally get a letter from you.*
>
> *Love, Katie*

I knew it had to be Dr. Newton grabbin' my letters to Katie. But, how could I tell her? I figured her pa just may also be readin' them, so in the next one I told Katie that I was writin' to Mr. Webster, Newton's Postmaster. Even Dr. Newton better not mess with the United States Postal Service! Anyhow, I

mailed both the letters that same day.
A week later I received:

> *Robby,*
>
> *It's now the two month anniverery since you left and still not a word from you. I walked out to Eloise's house yesterday and she told me she's received a bunch of letters from you. I'll just wait a while longer.*
>
> *Anyhow, I have some very important news for you. For starters, Crafton's not distributing fruit to anyone. I know because last weekend mom and dad and I went up to Talahassee for a day of shopping and on the way home stopped for gas in Clancy. I went into the grocery for a Dr. Pepper and asked the proprietor if he bought his fruit from Mr. Crafton. He told me he gets some local grown and some brought in by train once a week and delivered by truck. That's the same for all the little towns around. He's never heard anything about Crafton distributing any fruit.*
>
> *I believe you were right about Crafton after all; I think he was flying in bottling equipment, bottles, syrup, capping machine and whatever else he needed all camouflaged in fruit cardboard boxes in case anybody saw them being unloading. I'm going to need proof before I tell daddy that Crafton was a no good lier when he called you a sneakthief. I haven't figured out yet how to get it but I'll think of something.*
>
> *I just wish you were here. You'd figure out in a minute how to expose what Mr. Crafton's doing. I've got to leave for school now. Maybe today will be my lucky day to receive a letter.*

> *Affectionately,   Katie*

My heart was churnin' up the dust when I set the letter down. Katie was right. There was no honest reason Crafton was flying in big boxes of stuff into Newton before daylight. He simply didn't want nobody to see the stuff.

I was worried sick about what Katie might do. I didn't want her makin' no enemy outta Crafton. I knew just how mean the man could be. My gut told me to write Katie and tell her not to do nothin'. But, I knew that probably wasn't goin' to do me no good. She'd never get the letter. I hadn't heard back from Mr. Webster and suddenly realized he must be in cahoots with Dr. Newton.

Then I thought about Katie's part of the letter where she told me she'd been out to see Eloise. It dawned on my pea brain, that I could write Katie a letter and enclose it with a letter to Eloise! In Eloise's letter, I could ask her to meet Katie on her walk home from school and deliver my letter. I really hated to put Eloise in that spot, but I was desperate. I started my last letter to Katie that never got finished:

Dear Katie,

I've asked Eloise to deliver this letter to you on your way home from school. The reason is, I'm sure someone is getting my letters to you and I really need to tell you something.
Please don't do nothing about Crafton until you hear from me!
Anyhow, we're about to go on a field trip to Tybee Beach to look for sea animals like starfish and jelly fish for our biology class. As usual, the Sergeant is mean as a scorpion. He took away Rudy and my mail privileges for a week for no good reason and then told us we'd have to dig the field latrine today.

I dropped my pen when Rudy told me it was time to get on the bus.

"Where do you want it dug, Sergeant?" Rudy stood before Ellis with an army foldin' shovel in hand.

Ellis looked out to the furthest sand bar next to the softly lappin' Atlantic waves and pointed. "Out there where it will be washed out to sea when the tide comes in. See those pelicans?"

The other cadets, all dressed in their P.T. shorts, had removed their brogans and spread around a low-tide pond in their bare feet. Half of them was knee deep in the swirling' warm Atlantic water. They was tryin' to catch and bucket jellyfish. The others was gatherin' starfish.

Me and Rudy walked out across a gully that would be full of sea water at high-tide, and climbed onto the sand bar Ellis had pointed out for the field latrine.

In the early afternoon, the cadets took a lunch break of sandwiches and sodas the cooks had prepared for the trip. A little after four, Ellis told the cadets to make their final 'pit stop' of the day in the trench, and start wrapping' things up.

When the final cadet had returned from the sandbar, Ellis told me and Rudy to police the area for bottles and sandwich papers and then go fill the trench. The rest of the cadets was to add sea water to their starfish and jellyfish filled buckets and wait by the gravel road for the return of the Fort Pulaski bus.

"Move it, cadets," Ellis barked as he waded ankle deep in water through the previously dry sand and gravel covered gully. He climbed up the sand to where we was fillin' in the trench.

"What the hell is taking you so long?"

"Sorry Sergeant, moving as fast as we can," Rudy said.

"Well, make it faster. The bus will be here soon."

I looked up and saw sea water startin' to flow into the gully. "Reckon we'd better go on back now, Sergeant," I said.

"Afraid of a little water, McKinley?" Ellis smiled.

"No sir. but if you haven't noticed, there's sea weed all over this sand bar. I 'spect it'll be back under water pretty soon."

Ellis looked about the sand bar and replied, "There's plenty of time, Cadet. Just get on with filling the trench."

He sat on his haunches, leaned over, pushed together a small pillow of sand, and then laid down on his back with his hands behind his head and closed his eyes.

Me and Rudy scurried to a finish and ten minute later Rudy said, "We're ready to go, Sergeant."

We walked together down the sand bar. A wave broke, swashed in, licked the sandy bank and pulled back to reveal a narrow strip of dark sand. Ellis was stunned to see the gush of water pourin' into the gully.

"We'd better run for it!"

We jumped into the gully and got 'bout four good strides into it before the next wave reached us, calf deep. I could see the decision in Ellis' back and neck muscles as he lunged forward. The water was flowin' in like the closin' of the Red Sea after Moses' crossin'. There was no uncovered sand between us and the high gravel road ahead.

Before we got very far at all, the churnin' water was chest deep and we couldn't walk no more. I stumbled and went under, spittin' out briny sea water as I got to my feet.

I had fallen yards behind. With fifty feet to go, the water, now gushin' like a river, was up to our arm-pits. All the cadets on shore was yellin' at us.

"Help...help me! Ellis screamed, "I can't swim!"

He started thrashing about. I caught up with him and yelled, "Goldurnit! You can dog-paddle from here!"

Ellis was wild-eyed. "I'm gonna drown!"

"Damnit, paddle like a dog!"

Ellis flayed his arms and went under and I lost sight of him. I swam to where I'd seen him go under.

Rudy screamed, "Forget him, Rob!"

I dove and could barely make out the sergeant's flappin' body in the swirlin' brown water. I dove under him, grabbed an arm and surfaced, gaspin' for air. I tried treading water.

"I can get us both in if you'll relax!" I yelled into his ear.

Ellis was gaggin' and his eyes was bulgin'. He threw his arms around me and tried to climb right up onto my shoulders. For the first time, I was scar't and tried to pull him off.

He clawed all the harder to stand on top of me. My head was now beneath water. I guess Rudy came to my rescue 'bout then and got hold of the Sergeant's neck and pulled him off'a me. Ellis had pushed me under before I'd filled my lungs and I inhaled a mouth full of sea water. I retched and gagged and thought I was gonna die. It felt like red hot knives stuck into my lungs. I rolled onto my hands and knees, dug my toes into the sand and pushed myself gaggin' to the surface. I vomited and coughed out most of the water and got a blessin' of warm Georgia air into my lungs. I coughed and gagged between gulps of air. I looked around for Rudy and Ellis. I saw Rudy, one arm headlocked on Ellis and the other tryin' to dog- paddle them both to shore. Ellis was swingin' his arms around like a windmill.

I dove toward them to help but before I could get to them they went under. They come up again for a few seconds and I saw Rudy was still holdin' onto Ellis neck, and tryin' to swim like crazy. Ellis climbed right up Rudy's skinny body and they was under again. I took a deep breath and dove into the current where I'd last seen them. I couldn't see nothin' in the murky water. I came up to the screams of the boys jumpin' and yellin' on the bank. I took another huge gulp of air and dove again, swimmin' under water in circles.

Ellis' flayin' arm hit me right in the mouth. I dove away before he could grab me. I got under him, planted my feet in the sand, and pushed up on his butt until I knew his head was above water. I held him up as long as I could hold my breath, and then released him and pushed myself up for a breath.

Ellis slid 'neath the surface again, but he'd managed to gobble in a little air first. I took a quick look for Rudy and saw him crawlin' up the bank 'bout twenty feet downstream. I dove beneath Ellis a second time, planted my feet in the sand, and pushed him both up and in the direction of the shore. When I could no longer stay under, I let him go and went up for my own air. I swallowed a mouthful of air and dove again, repeatin' this maneuver of pushin' Ellis toward air and shore as long as I could hold my breath. He calmed a mite and must have realized what I was doin' and stopped fightin'.

After several more dive and pushes on Ellis' butt, my feet touched the gully floor while my head was still above water. I let Ellis stand and said, "Reckon we can walk from here."

As we climbed up the gully bank, we was surrounded by cheerin' cadets. I looked around for Rudy. I saw him lyin' on his face half out of the water right where I'd seen him draggin' himself out. I ran down the bank, grabbed his shoulders and turned him over. His eyes was rolled way back in his head and his face so drained of color it looked like a vampire had done sucked him dry.

Me and Ellis turned him over and pushed on his chest until sea water came spurtin' outta his mouth. Ellis carried him to the bus and we raced to Tybee clinic. I told the doctor there 'bout Rudy's heart murmur and he decided to keep Rudy there under observation for a few days.

That evening after lights out, Marvin Ellis slipped into my room. "You're one helluva guy, Rob McKinley," Ellis said.

"Thanks, Sergeant."

"Please call me Marvin, Rob. I want you to know I sure hope Rudy's alright."

"Me too," I replied.

Marvin kind'a did a slow shuffle and looked down at his feet. "And thanks for saving my life.

"Sure."

"I acted pretty stupid."

"That's alright, Marvin."

"Honest to God, I'da been a goner if you and Rudy hadn't been there." He turned to look at the wall. "I'll be sorry for the rest of my life for the way I treated you two."

"Why was you so hard on us?" I asked.

"The Major ordered it. He said Rudy's dad was a nothing more than a Cuban crook and your dad was, I'm sorry to tell you Rob, a drunken Florida Cracker. He told me it was up to him and me to protect the tradition of the Academy by drumming both of you out. I was to make it so tough on you, you'd have to both leave."

"My pa ain't no drunk." I bristled.

Marvin nodded. "I guess I ought'a get a move on. Is there anything I can do for you?"

"How about gettin' me my mail."

"Oh hell!" Ellis snapped his fingers and scooted out of the room.

Marvin returned a few minutes. "Here's your mail, Rob."

"Just the one letter?" My mouth dropped open.

"That's all there's been, Rob." Marvin shuffled his feet. "I'll be going back to my room. Let me know if there's anything else I can do for you."

I nodded and tore open the envelope.

Dear Robby,

Something awful has happened. Something I can't risk telling anyone but you about. Since daddy refuses to believe you're anything but a sneakthief, I decided it was going to be up to me to get the goods on Crafton and prove daddy wrong. So I waited until my parents were asleep last night and then snuck out to Crafton's barn. As I was getting close, I heard two men talking around the side of the barn. I tiptoed close enough to hear some of their conversation and ducked down behind Crafton's pickup. I could see it was Crafton talking with a big, mean-looking man. They were talking about a business plan.

Crafton said, "You've been gone a long time. What's the condition of your equipment?"
The man told him, "It needed some parts."

Crafton asked him, "Where'd you get money for parts?"
The man answered, "My old buddy, Bill Dooley, loaned me what I needed."

Crafton said, "Rusty mentioned you was with Dooley at the last couple of pick-ups."

I couldn't make out what they were saying for a few minutes and then heard Crafton say, "So, you want in on our little operation do you?"

The man said, "As long as only you and Rusty know I'm in this part of the woods."

Crafton said, "And, of course, Dooley."

I couldn't make out the next part of the conversation, but then heard the man ask, "How many of us are involved?"

Crafton said, "Anyone who knows the business and wants in."

They talked a bit more but their voices were again too low for me to hear. Then, Crafton said pretty loud, "I got to get back to work. I'll tell Rusty to fly over your neck of the woods during the day of the pick-up. That's the signal for you, Dooley and Zitterkopf to meet him at the pick-up and delivery point after the moon comes up."

The man agreed and then Crafton added, "Don't come back around here again, it's too risky."

With that, Crafton scooted back into the barn and closed the door. I heard a lock-bar slam into place. I expected the man to head toward the path that would take him back to town. I was stunned when, instead, he came right toward me as if he was heading to the river. Straight away he spotted me. I screamed and took off running. He was very fast and caught me before I got very far.

He grabbed me up and said, "You shouldn't be spying, little lady." He held me by my neck and pulled me right into his face.

"Just a pity, you being such a pretty little thing," he said and pushed me down on my back and put both his hands around my neck.

Thank God, Crafton came out of the barn just then and grabbed the big man by the shoulder and pulled on him and said,

"What are you doing, you fool? You're going to kill her!"

The man said, "That's my intention."

Crafton said, "This here's the doctor's girl, you idiot!"

The man answered, "She saw me. I cain't afford to have

no one know I've been here. I'm going to snap this pretty little neck. Don't worry none. I'll lose her in the swamp."

Crafton said, "Not if you want to be part of this operation you won't." And he pulled on the man some more.

The man shook his head. "Sorry, I just cain't take the risk."

In the moonlight, Crafton was now shaking a little and he stepped back and yanked a gun out of his pocket and pointed it right at the man and said, "You're not killin' nobody! Not on my property. Now listen to me. She don't know you and I never used your name. You're paranoid, man. You don't up and kill a girl just because she heard us talking a little reckless."

The big man just kept on holding me loosely by my neck and staring Crafton down.

Crafton was now holding the gun in both hands and they were shaking like he had the palsy. He said, "You don't let her go, I'm going to shoot."

With that, the big man slowly let go of me. He stood up and towered over Crafton. Crafton backed off and said, "Now get on home, I'll take care of this with the doctor. You won't have no problem."

"It's on your head if I do," the man said.

Crafton chewed on his lower lip and said, "The doctor'll believe what I tell him."

The big man pointed a finger at Crafton. "If you cain't handle this, have Rusty tell me on his next pick up."

Crafton shuddered, "If I have a problem, Rusty will tell you. That's a promise."

The man then smiled as mean as the devil and turned to me, put his dirty index finger on my nose and whispered, "You tell anybody about this night and I'm gonna snap your pretty little neck like a chicken's and feed you to the 'gators. And that's a fact."

Crafton looked at me real stern and said, "He means it, Katie. You best listen real close to what you just heard the man say. If you tell your pa or anyone, I won't be there next time to protect you."

I was awake most of the night shaking and crying and waiting for daylight. In the morning, daddy stormed into my room as mad as I've ever seen him. Before I could say anything, he said he'd had a call from Crafton telling him I'd been sneaking around his place just like that sneakthief, Robby McKinley. Crafton told him I may have overheard an argument him and a new part-time employee were having but to pay no attention to anything I might have heard. They'd been a little hot under the collar because they'd been drinking.

I started to cry and tried to interrupt but daddy put up his hand and told me he knew I was determined to try to clear your name, but it was too late for that. The Academy would get you back on track and I was not to worry mom or tell anyone about getting caught sneaking around Mr. Crafton's private property. He said he was ashamed of me, told me to get ready for school and stormed out of the room. Robby, I'm scared to death of that big man. It wasn't just a drunken argument I overheard. I'm convinced that the whole lot of them, the man, Crafton, Yates, Dooley and Zitterkopf plus maybe a bunch of others are in a conspiracy to take over daddy's business. But, if I try to get daddy to listen to me when he calms down, I know he's not going to believe the man was serious in his intentions. And if daddy did talk to Crafton about the threat and asked him who the big man was, Crafton's going to tell the man about it. Crafton's too afraid of the man not to. Then the man will come after me. I sure wish you were here.
Love, Katie

I rolled over on my bunk and moaned.

CHAPTER 9

Marvin's Story Continued:

The morning after I gave Rob his letter, I told the Squad to 'fall in' just outside the front door to R barracks. I called them to attention in preparation to march to the chow hall. Rob wasn't in the formation.

"Parade rest!" I called out and murmured to the guys in the front row, "I'll be right back."

I ran up the steps and trotted down to room R9. Rob was lying on his back with his arms behind his head. He was staring vacantly at the ceiling.

"How ya doin', buddy?" I said.

He slowly dropped his head and looked at me with absolutely no expression on his face. He didn't answer.

"You look bad, Rob. Let me take you to the Infirmary."

He looked back at the ceiling without any change in expression.

I said, "I'll cover for you." I thought for a minute. "Can I bring you something from the mess?"

He shook his head while studying the ceiling. I noticed his face looked drained of blood and his eyes were puffy.

"Stay in bed. I'll be back at lunch and see if there's anything I can do." I backed out of the room. Rob wasn't tall on esprit de corps but he sure wasn't short on guts.

I couldn't concentrate on the morning classes. At lunch, I made a sandwich from the food off my tray and stuffed it and a carton of milk into my jacket and hustled off to Rob's room. His door was shut.

"Rob?" I tapped the door lightly.

He didn't answer. I slowly opened the door and peeked in. Rob was standing at the mirror adjusting a pair of civilian jeans. They were an inch too short and tight around the middle.

"What are you doing, Rob?"

"Goin' home."

"In those clothes? Where'd you get 'em?"

"My girl needs me," he said.

"Tell me about it," I said and he did.

"Whoa," I said. "Your girlfriend has overheard a conspiracy to put her dad out of business involving a guy threatening to kill her if she tells her father or anybody else that she's even seen him."

He nodded and started pulling down the blankets on his bed. I paused and thought for a minute. "You know, Rob, it probably was just an idle drunken threat and the bully was just enjoying scaring a young girl."

"And if it wasn't?" Rob looked at me over his shoulder.

I thought for a minute longer. "Why not call your dad and let him handle it? He looked pretty capable to me."

"We ain't got no phone for one. The only place I can talk to my pa is at his job and Crafton would answer the phone. He's pa's boss and would guess straight away I was callin' because Katie'd written me about the threat." He turned back to pulling down the covers and then turned back to me. "Besides, pa wouldn't take Katie's letter serious. He'd just be pissed we was writin' to each other. What with her bein' the plant's owner's daughter."

I thought over Rob's predicament and searched for another solution, but I couldn't find one. Nobody here, particularly not the Major, would take this stuff seriously.

"How about you calling the doctor?" I asked.

Rob said, "He'd talk to Crafton straight away, and if Katie's right, Crafton will tell the big guy."

I asked, "What can you do to help her?"

Rob answered, "Find out what's goin' on in that barn and then show my pa. He'll take care of the rest."

After a minute more, I nodded. "You're doing the right thing, But, the Major's going to be after you hot and heavy the minute he finds out you're gone. He'll have to cover his butt."

"So?" Rob said.

"So, I'll think of something to throw him off long enough for you to get home."

"I'd 'preciate that, Marvin."

I pointed at his poorly fitted clothes. "You'll never get past the Sergeant-of -the-Guard in civvies, Rob, and, he'd see you if you tried jumping the fence."

"What do you think I ought'a do?"

"Wait until the study hour tonight. I'll visit the S.O.G. and keep him busy while you slip out. I won't report you missing until morning."

"Thanks, Marvin."

At seven that evening, I rapped on Rob's door. He was waiting dressed in fatigues.

"Where are your civvies?"

Under my fatigues."

I glanced at his bunk. "Who's sleeping in your bed?"

"About a dozen towels."

I took a close look at his bunk. Sure enough, it was towels but at a glance it looked every bit like somebody lying there with covers pulled up over his head. That made me smile. I said, "If you're ready, let's do it."

We walked casually out of the barracks and meandered toward the front gate. I kept up a meaningless line of chatter to make it look like we were having a one-on-one chat.

Within several yards of the front gate, I looked around to see if anyone was looking at us and then whispered, "Rob, get behind that tree. I'll get Wilkes, he's the S.O.G. tonight, to look the other way. When he does, you slip out the gate. I'll try to join you if I can." I was so damn nervous. "Wait for me fifteen minutes down at the Mom and Pop grocery at the crossroads."

He nodded and walked calm as anything over to the tree and disappeared. I was stretched fiddle-tight and marched on out to the gate with my chest pushed out. "Evening, Sergeant Wilkes."

"Evening to you, Sergeant Ellis. What's up?"

"I'm heading down to the Mom and Pop for a Coke."

Wilkes shook his head on a long skinny neck. "Marvin, you know the S.O.G can't let anyone through after sunset."

I slapped him on his narrow shoulders and laughed, "That rule's meant for recruits, not sergeants like us."

"Well, I don't know." Wilkes hesitated. As Rob would say, Wilkes had no more backbone than a snake has hips.

"I'll do the same thing for you when I'm on duty."
I punched him lightly on his upper arm. "I'm thirsty for one of their cherry cokes poured over shaved ice."

Wilkes paused. "Okay, this time. But make it snappy."

I jerked my head and pointed toward the grove of pines just beyond the gate. "What's that?"

Wilkes jumped off his stool, now alert, and looked where I'd pointed. "What's what?"

"Hell, I think I just saw a bobcat run through those trees."

"No crap? Where?" Wilkes squinted into the woods.

"I don't see nothin'."

I saw Rob dart through the gate.

I studied the pines for a minute more and sighed, "I guess I was mistaken." I turned back toward the road and winked at

Wilkes. "Be back soon ... and thanks." I sauntered on out the gate.

"How do you plan on getting home?" I asked Rob. "Do you have any money?" We were standing in front of the little grocery.

"No. I'll hitch-hike. I know where Newton is on the map."

"A kid your age hitch-hiking will attract the Highway Patrol's attention straight out. I think you'd be better off hopping a train."

"Like the hobos do?" He grinned.

I had twenty dollars I planned on giving him and wondered how far he could get with that on a bus. I discounted that idea knowing the Major would have a bus checked first thing. I had an idea. "The freights going south to Valdosta slow for traffic at a signal over on Highway 80. I hear a whistle about eight every evening."

Rob smiled. "Valdosta, Georgia is just across the border from Florida and not too far from Newton." He slapped me lightly on my back. "Which way is it to Highway 80?"

"I'll take you and help you get aboard."

"You'll get busted if you aren't back by lights out. I can find the tracks without you."

"Wilkes isn't going to blow the whistle on me and if we hustle I can make it back for lights out." I started trotting away from the grocery. "Come on."

A half hour later, we arrived at the traffic signal and looked up and down the track.

"We've got a few minutes before the train comes, Rob."

He took off his fatigues and dropped them by the tracks.

I thrust the twenty dollar bill into his hand. "Here, I want you to have this."

He shoved it back. "I can't take that."

"The hell you can't. You don't know where you're going to end up. It may be days before you get home. You've got

71

to eat."

He pocketed the bill. "Thanks Marvin."

"I wish I had more."

I dropped to my knees and put an ear to the track. I looked up at Rob. "It's coming."

Rob was shifting his weight from foot to foot as I stood up.

"Look Rob, the train starts slowing down about a quarter mile up the track. It comes through this intersection fairly slow, but it doesn't stop. We're going to have to run along side and find you a car to get on. I'll give you a boost up."

Rob nodded his head. I saw beads of sweat on his upper lip. A train whistle pierced the night and the slowing train suddenly materialized from around the bend.

"Start running, Rob!" Anxiety tickled my belly.

The roar of the train was suddenly upon us as the diesel engine rumbled past. Looking over our shoulders as we ran, we saw an empty flat bed followed by three freight cars with a caboose bringing up the rear. Rob tugged at my sleeve and pointed to the flat bed. Shaking my head, I jerked a thumb toward the freights.

The first one came along side. I tried the sliding door handle and was nearly jerked off my feet. I stumbled in the pea gravel and crushed rock beside the track, but regained my footing.

The second car was suddenly upon us. I grabbed another locked door lightly and let go. Rob looked at me with wild eyes as the third car came adjacent to us. We were both gasping for air. He grabbed a door ajar and jerked. The door slid away. I reached down and grabbed him with one hand by the seat of his pants and the other by the back of his flannel shirt and shoved up with all of my might. At the same time, Rob put both hands on either side of the open doorway and jumped. He hurtled into the black interior of the car and slid along an oil slick dark wooden surface on his face and hands.

I skidded to a stop in the gravel and watched Rob climb up and stand in the open doorway as the train picked up speed. He waved at me. It made my stomach churn. He looked so damn young and alone standing there in pants a bunch too small for him. I knew he had to be scared shitless about what he was doing, but he waved a second time real cool like. I realized right then I was looking at a very special person and waved like crazy back at him.

I looked after the train long after it was out of sight. Then, I gathered up Rob's fatigues and headed back to the Academy.

As I was approaching the Mom and Pop, I saw Wilkes come slammimg out through the screen door. He stopped, put his hands on his hips, and looked both ways. Before he turned toward me, I threw Rob's fatigues behind a bush.

"Where in hell have you been?" He yelled at me. I waited until I got a little closer and then answered, "It's such a nice evening I decided to take a little walk."

His eyebrows climbed right up his forehead and his voice squeeked, "Taking a little walk? You dog poop for brains, are you crazy? I could get busted for letting you out after sundown."

I forced a laugh and slapped him on the back. "You'll get busted for sure if you don't get back to your post. Come on, we better hustle."

We started to trot back up the road with him bitching at me all the way. We saw the Savannah Laundry Service truck pull through the Academy gate as it does every evening at this time. Its driver turned on the headlights and accelerated toward us. We jumped behind an old Oak tree until it had passed and a plan to help Rob suddenly popped into my head.

CHAPTER 10
Rob's Story Continued:

I jumped to my feet and stood in the open doorway lookin' back at a wavin' Marvin Ellis. I returned the wave and watched his figure fade off in the distance.

I turned and looked into the car and was startled to see a figure lyin' in a darkened corner under a deep blue Navy P coat. An empty green bottle slid toward me as the train accelerated around a bend in the tracks. With a poundin' heart, I was suddenly surrounded in an inky darkness as I slid the door shut. With the door shut, I heard the guy in the corner snorin' and coughing like an overture at a funeral. I reeled around the other end of the car a bit like a pup trying to find a spot to lie down knowin' I'd never get to sleep.

I awakened to a screechin' and clangin' like I'd never heard before and jumped up from the freight car floor. The figure I'd found sleepin' in the corner a few hours before was standin' in the open doorway of the stationary freight car lookin' out as the train pulled away. A mountain in a P coat and dirty blue and white stripped overalls.

"What's goin' on?" I asked.

The man turned and stared at me with black eyes surrounded by weathered leathery skin from too much sun or alcohol.

"What're you'all doin' here, kid?" His breath was strong enough to crack a mirror.

"I'm tryin' to get home to Newton, Florida. "Where are we? Why, is the train leavin'?"

"Newton, Florida?" The man's dark high cheek-boned face was a mass of friendly wrinkled flesh as it split into a smile.

"When, pray tell, did you'all get in this car and where did you think it was going?"

I studied him for a minute. "I jumped aboard in Savannah. You was asleep. I figured we might stop in Valdosta."

The man started to laugh which sent him into a coughin' fit. His whiskey breath was certainly no perfume from France. He took several deep breaths and dropped heavily to the track below. He looked strong enough to derail a freight train.

"May as well get out." He looked at me with a kindly grimace and absentmindedly rumpled his mop of hair with one hand and rattled change in his pocket with the other. "This old car ain't going nowhere."

I climbed down and looked around in the early morning light. I saw we was standin' on one of half a dozen parallel tracks with tall, coarse, blue-green grass growin' heavily between them. The high ground was covered in pine trees and the lower surroundin' ground was part bog and swamp. Several of the tracks held old freight and flat cars that appeared to have not moved in ages. An ancient looking dirty-yellow engine was parked next to an unpainted oak and cypress shed with a rusted tin roof. The air smelled of trees, wet moss and damp earth.

"Where are we?" I repeated.

"Well, we ain't in Newton, son. But not too far as the crow flies." The man put out a dirty hand the size of a country ham. "My name's Mordecai, but most people call me Smokey.

What's yours?

I told him and received a knuckle-poppin' handshake.

"What kind of a place is this?" I asked.

Smokey started walking toward the shed and waved for me to follow. His overalls was baggy and flapped as he strode across the tracks.

"It's a switching yard, or used to be. Doesn't get much use anymore."

I stumbled across the series of tracks. "What's a switchin' yard?"

"Where an engineer makes up a train. Cars are assigned to the district they's goin' to end up for whatever loads need to be moved. This switching yard's now mostly used to store worn-out cars until they can be recycled through a repair depot."

Smokey stopped in front of a rusty caboose just beyond the shed. "Here's home."

He opened a door and gestured me in. I hesitated and looked through the doorway. I saw that the car had been outfitted with a wood stove, table and two chairs, and an army cot covered in a stained blue blanket.

"You live here?"

"I'm kind'a a retired engineer. They let me live in this old caboose the last few weeks in exchange for keeping an eye on things." He was quiet for a moment and then spoke again, "They also bring me home whenever I fall off the wagon and get drunker'n a Shriner." His face colored and the skin at the corner of his mouth tugged slightly into a smile.

"You mean that entire train came out here to just drop you off?" I stepped into the caboose.

Smokey laughed, "This time they had to drop off that beat up car we were in. The engineer's my buddy. He pulled me out'ta a Charleston dive where I was fixin' to get into a fight." Smokey chuckled a little more. "I'd been drinking 'shine likker strong enough to make a rabbit jump a wolf and was snot slingin' drunk."

I shook my head and Smokey pointed me toward a chair. He said, "Let's see what I can rustle up for us to eat."

He moved to a cupboard and looked in.

"How about some black olives and prunes?"

He turned around and waved a can in each hand beamin' like he was the chef of a fancy French restaurant.

I sat down and grinned. "Sure. Haven't had those two for breakfast in awhile."

Smokey found a can opener, a couple of paper plates, and two stained forks while I asked him, "Where'd you get the 'shine likker? Is it easy to get ahold of?" Smokey shook his head, "Not usually, but a buddy told me about a soft drink distributor up in Valdosta that's started sellin' it the last few weeks to the family grocers in all the little towns around. They order up their usual cases of soda pop along with a case or two of 'shine on the side in the same kind'a cases."

"That's illegal, ain't it?"

"A little, I suppose, but worth the risk for the profits. A 'shiner can make a gallon of good 'shine for probably fifty cents. Where a gallon of legal whiskey would cost goin' on thirty bucks or more. So, a 'shiner can probably sell it to the distributor for a few bucks and make a helluva profit. The distributor and then the grocer can all have huge markups and still sell it for a lot less than legal whiskey."

"Why is legal whiskey so expensive?" I asked.

"Why, 'cause over half the price is government tax, and that's a fact. Losin' that tax income is the only reason the government gives a hoot 'bout shuttin' down the 'shiners. Moonshine is a blessin' for those of us as poor as a hind-tit calf. That ain't no lie."

While I thought on what I'd just heard, Smokey served up our breakfast. After a couple of bites he wiped his mouth on the back of his sleeve and asked while spitting out a prune pit, "How come you aboard that train?"

I told him my story.

"Well I'll be a suck-egg mule! Smokey exclaimed. "What're you gonna do 'bout it all when you get home?" He lit a cigarette and started to clear the table.

"I'm gonna find out once and for all what's goin' on in that barn. When I've got the proof Crafton's havin' equipment flown in and is hirin' employees on the sly, I'll give it to pa and the doctor."

Smokey looked up at the ceiling and blew smoke through his nostrils. "I got a cousin what married a guy named Crafton down in Newton 'bout fifteen years ago. Met him once't. Didn't like him." Smokey nodded. "Anyhow, your plan sounds the reasonable thing to do. But why not have your pa go with you to the barn?"

"He wouldn't do it. Crafton's his boss. Pa'd just be more pissed than ever at me for runnin' off from the Academy and breakin' his rules to stay away from Crafton's. No, I know how to sneak up close this time and not get caught."

While Smokey mulled that over, I asked, "Can I ask why you live here?" I waved my hand around.

He set his cigarette on the end of the table. "Son, I was raised right out there where God created the Garden of Eden." He pointed out the window. "This is as close to home as I can get without a boat."

"Garden of Eden?" I asked, "A swamp?"

Smokey slowly shook his shaggy head. "It's full'a water moccasins and 'gators, all right. But there's nothing like it anywhere I've been; it smells of part resin, part watery mud, part tang and part sweetness. And you don't hear nothing except unimaginable silence until maybe a flock of migratory birds swoosh in." He paused in thought. "It's heaven to some, maybe hell to others." He shrugged his shoulders.

I said, "You must be a Seminole." I remembered Eloise's lecture.

"You right as rain, boy." Smokey turned and smiled with eyes as bright as seed pods. "I'm part Seminole and part black ...

78

as you can probably see." He chuckled.

I asked, "You said I'm close to home?"

Smokey answered, "I said as the crow flies, or I should say as the alligator swims. Newton in about fifteen miles due south right through there." He pointed out into the trees. "But, it's forty miles around it by train. Probably over a hundred by road."

"Can I get through?" I pointed into the pine forest. I could distinguish the dry green pinelands from the damp forest hammocks and swamps.

Smokey slowly shook his head. "I could, but not you. And that's a fact."

I hitched up my trousers. "Why not me?"

Smokey looked into his now empty food cupboard and replied, "I'll show you." He pulled down a stub of a pencil and a folded brown paper bag. He spread the bag on the table and made a sketch.

"There's nothing 'twix here and Newton but a maze of canals and bayous most of which are choked with water lilies and tall grass. Where there's not water there's marshes and ham-mocks."

I studied the drawing. "Where did 'ja live?"

"Just a couple'a miles south, 'bout here." Smokey pointed. "The swamp is so damn dense there, nobody'd ever see the house if they didn't know it was there."

"Why'd you leave?" I asked.

"Ma died when my brother Luke was borned. Pa was a moonshiner. He up and drowned out fishin' one day with Luke when Luke was 'bout fifteen. Luke and I never did get along, so I up and left. Joined the railroad and learned to drive a train."

"What happeened to your brother?"

"He took over pa's 'shine business 'till he got busted 'bout a dozen years ago." Smokey said.

"Busted?"

"He's crazy as popcorn on a hot skillet. Somebody stole

his rudder before he was borned. He's been in the state prison for the last twelve years for gut knifin' a second rate 'shiner from your part of the woods." Smokey pointed at me. "A guy named Jesse Brown what lived near Newton but kept a still deep in the swamp."

"Brown?" I said, "Was he married to Eloise Brown?"

"He was a half-breed like me and married to some black gal, but I don't know her name. I heard Luke was pissed at havin' the competition and cut Jesse up and left him for dead. Luke's plumb soft north of the ears and thinks he can solve any problem by killin'. Jesse was able to get his boat back to his shack during the night but was too weak to climb outta it. His wife found him in the mornin' lying in a pool'a blood in the bottom of the boat. He told her it was Luke what killed him and he then up and died in her arms."

Smokey clenched a fist and shoved a thumb into the air. "It was her testimony what put Luke away."

"I reckon that was Eloise Brown. She's a good friend of mine."

Smokey shrugged his shoulders. "I heard Jesse's woman was a fine lady, but Jesse was so lazy he had nothin' to do but stand around and scratch his butt. But he didn't deserve to die."

Smokey shook his head. "My bother'd lose an I.Q. contest with a stump, I swear. There warn't no reason for him to kill ol' Jesse. There's no real money in bein' a 'shiner in the middle of the swamp when the only way in and out is poling a flat-bottom boat."

"Why's that?" I asked.

"Cause a motorboat's propeller gets caught up in all the saw grass, rush an' stuff. It was a three day round trip for Luke just to get from his still to Newton and back. Newton's where he sold most his 'shine a bottle at a time. But, he's one 'a them psychos you hear about. Just loves to hurt people. My earliest recollection of him is pullin' the wings off'a flies."

I asked, "Will he ever get outta prison?"

Smokey shook his head. "The damn fool up and broke the neck of a fellow inmate a few years back. He's now servin' two life sentences in a maximum security cell."

I choked that one down and then Smokey nodded slowly. "Rob, you stay outta that swamp. Even I'd get lost if I didn't know one canal from another."

"There's no way I can walk through?" I asked.

"What little solid ground there is is thick with moss covered cypress and pine trees. You'd get lost within minutes and never find your way out."

I hitched up my trousers again. "Then I'd better get goin'. I've got a forty mile walk ahead." I pushed out my right hand.

"Thanks for the hospitality, Smokey."

Smokey stood there, airin' his paunch and raised a hand to the policeman's halt position. "You fixin' to walk the tracks out'ta here?"

I shoved both hands into trouser pockets. "Yep."

Smokey inhaled taking his time on how to answer. He shrugged and let out his breath. "Oh hell, kid, I've got a headache built for a horse. I hoped I could just crash on this cot for a couple of days ... but let's see if I can't you to Newton. Come on."

He swung the caboose door open and walked toward the shed. I stopped to fold up the paper bag and stuffed it into my trouser pocket. I skipped to catch up to him.

"What'cha doin', Smokey?"

"I'm going to see if I can get this old switching engine running and take you home."

Smokey opened the shed door and rummaged through a large and splintered wooden box and found what he was looking for. I kept a close eye on what he was doing. Smokey folded up a track map and stuffed it in his shirt pocket.

He then picked up several handles and what appeared to be a key of some sort with a screwdriver type handle and stuffed them into his overall pockets. He walked toward the edge of the yard and stopped beside a black dirt and oil covered metal container bolted to two railroad ties. He grabbed a large handle and pulled it up.

"What'cha doin', Smokey?"

"Changing the outgoing track to the Clancy-Newton feeder."

Smokey walked on to the diesel he'd referred to as a switching engine, grabbed a metal rail, and swung up the rusty steps and into the cab.

I followed him in and watched as he squatted on his haunches in front of a red container in the forward left side of the cab and opened a door.

"What's in there?" I leaned over his shoulder and peered in.

"The main battery and mag switches. They've both gotta be on before I can try to crank this old girl."

Smokey closed the door and moved to the engineer's seat on the right side of the cab. He shoved the key into a slot.

"What are those handles you're holdin', Smokey?"

"This one goes here on the reverser." He slid it into place.

"The engineer always locks up these controls so's no one else can start his engine."

Smokey turned to a platform to his left and slid the final two handles into place.

"This handle on top controls the engine's brakes. The one below controls the train's brakes."

I pursed my lips. "This engine don't look a lot like the ones that come into Newton."

"Not as big," Smokey agreed. "It's just used to move cars 'round to make up a train here in the switching yard."

"What are those switches and meters in front of you, Smokey?"

"This one's for the engine's fuel pump." He flicked it on. "Gotta build up ten pounds of pressure before I try to start the engine."

Smokey pushed on a button on the lower left of the control panel labeled "starter" and I heard the engine slowly turn over.

"We're in luck." He looked up at me standin' beside him. "The batteries still gotta little juice."

After several rotations, I heard the low rumble of a runnin' diesel engine.

Smokey yelled above the noise, "Got to let her warm up until we get seventy pounds of air pressure for the brakes before we can go."

My eyes opened wide. "Is that all there is to startin' a train?"

"You're durn tootin'." Smokey reached over and released a parking brake, turned and pushed the reverser handle into the forward position. I saw that it only had three positions forward, reverse and neutral.

"Let's take you'all home!" Smokey yelled and shoved the throttle forward. The train slowly accelerated out of the yard.

We was soon sailin' down the track with the right hand window open and Smokey's curly black hair was blowin' in the breeze. Within minutes, we could see a town in the distance of clapboard and screened beer joints, a grocery and a hardware store. Smokey pulled the track map out of his shirt pocket and studied it for a few minutes. He hooked an index finger to draw me over to look at the map.

"That's Smithtown. It's on the main track heading north to Valdosta," Smokey yelled above the drone and clickety-clack of the train. "I'm going east on this dead end feeder track into Clancy and Newton." He traced a finger across the map. "It's only used 'bout once a week when a little freight picks up goods from Newton."

I cocked an ear and Smokey put a cupped hand to his mouth and yelled, "I'm glad 'cause I'd hate to see a big diesel electric coming at us full throttle! Probably cause me to let go in my pants." He laughed for a moment and then turned his head toward me. "I can drop you at your doorstep."

I shook my head and yelled back, "We'd cause too much attention. I'd rather get off just before Clancy and walk the seven miles on into Newton."

Forty minutes later, Smokey reviewed the map again and said, "I think we're just about there."

He reduced the throttle by several indents and proceeded to pump the upper brake handle. When the engine slowed to idling, Smokey reached out and shook my hand real formal like. "You're quite a lad, Rob. If things don't go well for you, come back to the caboose. I'll help you anyway I can."

I gave him a Fort Pulaski salute. "Thanks."
I climbed down the louvered metal steps and turned and waved. A smile winnowed up over Smokey's wrinkled mouth. I noticed for the first time several small scars on his face where his two or three day growth of beard wasn't growing. It crossed my mind that he was probably the toughest lookin' dude I'd ever seen. Smokey slapped the reverser handle through neutral and into reverse. The engine slowly accelerated back the way it had come.

Gray thunderhead clouds was rollin' in from the south. A breeze kicked up smellin' of plowed earth. I pushed my hands deep into my pant's pockets and walked the last quarter mile into Clancy.

Clancy was a farmin' village built around a townsquare. The single cafe had a Confederate flag flyin' over its door. I entered and found I was the only customer. I sat down at a red checkered linoleum covered table, pulled Marvin's crumpled twenty dollar bill out of my pocket, spread it out on the table, and looked up into the eyes of a tired, middle aged waitress with a slack face as wrinkled as a burnt boot.

"I'd like scrambled eggs with country ham and grits, ma'am." I said as hungry as a woodpecker with a headache.

CHAPTER 11
Marvin's Story Continues:

After lights out, I did my rounds of bed checks. None of the cadets had missed Rob during the evening. Billy Oglethorpe mentioned he'd knocked at R9 earlier in the evening and then stuck his head in the door. "Rob was already asleep with the covers pulled over his head," Billy said.

After slipping into R9, I quietly laid both chairs on their sides on the floor and shoved the table around at an odd angle; grabbed the pile of towels out from under the covers and as an after thought dropped Rob's most recent homework papers on the floor. I checked that the coast was clear in the hallway and returned the towels to the supply closet and went to bed.

After marching the troops to breakfast in the morning, I went directly to the Major's office.

"Major Swagart, Cadet McKinley was missing at roll call this morning and his room's empty."

The Major gave a wolfish grin. "So the little hillbilly has finally packed it in."

"I think maybe he was abducted, sir." I described the condition of R9.

The Major slammed his chair back and raced aroud his desk. "Show me," he said.

A few minutes later, the Major, with his fists on his hips, surveyed R9. He turned to me and whispered, "Keep the lid on this for now until I can find out what in hell is going on."

"Yes sir."

"If he has been abducted, the other parents are going to panic and start taking their sons home. It could ruin the Fort."

He made his right hand into a fist and shook it at the window.

"I knew nothing good was going to come from letting the riff-raff into the Academy. I'm already hearing the repercussions from some of the parents who've learned the Romero boy is having heart trouble after almost drowning. I don't want anymore problems. No siree, not on my watch." He scurried about the room, righting the chairs and tidying up. "Who was SOG last night?"

"Sergeant Wilkes was, sir," I answered.

"Pull him out of class and have him in my office in five minutes."

"What's up?" Wilkes was white as a sheet as we double timed to the Major's office.

"The Major just told me to get you."

"Oh shit, does he know I let you go out after sunset?"

"No."

"Do you think he knows I left my post to go hunt for you?"

"I don't know."

"Oh shit," Wilkes repeated.

"Stand at Parade Rest, Sergeant Wilkes." The Major was sitting behind his desk and was pointing his swagger stick at the two of us. "You were SOG last night. Did you let any vehicles come on our grounds on your watch?"

"No sir." Wilkes squeaked.

"Not even the daily laundry truck?"

"Oh, I let it pass sir." Wilkes shifted his weight from foot to foot. "May I ask why you're asking, sir?"

"You sure as hell cannot and stand at attention if you can't stop fidgeting!" The Major threw up his hands in exasperation.

The Major turned to me. "Did you see any other vehicles?"

"No sir."

"Wilkes, did you let any cadets pass through the gate last night?"

After a long hesitation, Wilkes squeaked again, "No sir."

The Major waved his stick at him. "Okay, you're dismissed, Sergeant. Get back to your classroom."

As soon as Wilkes shot out of the room, the Major focused his steely eyes on me. "Something damned strange is going on here, Ellis. R9 looks like McKinley was involved in quite a struggle, and yet none of the other boys reported hearing anything?"

"No sir."

"Did any of the boys see McKinley during the evening?"

I told him about Billy Oglethorpe's visit to Rob's room.

"Then he was already in bed by lights out. You know, he could have just run for it and messed up his room to throw us off."

The Major was nodding his head and mostly talking to himself. "He couldn't have gotten past Wilkes without being seen. Unless he snapped his fingers. "Unless he hid in the back of the laundry truck." The Major reached for the telephone. "You can sit down, Ellis. We've got to get to the bottom of this immediately."

For the next few minutes, I sat in agony listening to the Major's half of a conversation with the laundry truck driver.

"Thank you, very much," the Major said and set the phone

into its cradle. He exploded, "Get that miserable little bastard back in here. On the double!"

I thought Wilkes was going to faint when I pulled him out of class the second time. He totally fell apart as soon as the Major told him the laundry truck driver said he'd been very surprised to find no SOG at the gate either coming or going.

"I'm sorry, sir. I just left my post for a few minutes to get a coke at the Mom and Pop."

You don't need to hear the ranting and raving that came out of the Major's mouth after that. After a bit, he busted Wilkes to recruit on the spot and told him to get out of his sight.

The Major regained his composure doing some deep breathing after Wilkes was gone. He asked, "Do you think the hillbilly's made a run for it?"

"No, sir."

"Well I do." He frowned. "The laundry truck driver said he'd of seen anybody inside of his truck in the rear view mirror, but that little hillbilly didn't need to be that smart. Not with Wilkes leaving the gate unattended." The Major looked toward the ceiling and posed his hands together like he was praying. "And, why in hell would anyone want to kidnap poor white trash?" He dropped his hands to his desk. "He's run for it." He cocked his head toward the ceiling. "Did you notice if his uniform was missing?"

"None of his hanging clothes were disturbed." I squirmed a little more in the hard backed wooden chair.

"Then he's dressed in fatigues. Well, he's not going to get far in them. I'm going to ask the Highway Patrol and Savannah police to be on the lookout for one of our boys around town dressed in fatigues." He pointed his swagger stick almost into my nose. "You're not to tell the other cadets. When they ask where McKinley is, tell them he's gone home for a family thing." The Major looked at the ceiling again like he'd just had another bout of inspiration. "You know, Ellis, it would have made a lot more sense if it had been the Romero boy being grabbed. After he was let into the Fort, I did some checking up on my own on his father. It turns out 'daddy' owns a fishing fleet all right, but he didn't make his money catching fish. He made it running Cuban wetbacks into Florida."

He dropped his head and gave me another piercing stare. "Let's give it a few days. Nobody's going to miss our hillbilly cadet. He'll come crawling back."

I was damned happy to get out of that office, I'll tell you. I didn't hear or see hide nor hair of the Major for the next two days. Then, I was called out of class to double time to his office again.

When I entered the room, I knew something big time had happened. "Close the door, Ellis," the Major whispered, "and pull your chair over close". I did as I was told.

"He's been kidnapped." The Major whispered.

"You mean, Rob?"

"Who in hell else, man!" He stopped whispering. "Of course I mean McKinley."

He stood up and walked around his desk and stood over me. The police just called. Somebody walking to the Mom and Pop found McKinley's stenciled fatigues behind a bush next to the road. The kidnappers changed him into street clothes just outside our gate, the arrogant bastards!"

I argued just to cover my part in the whole disappearance thing, "But you said there was no reason for anyone to kidnap a poor kid."

"You're right. But the kidnappers didn't know it was the wrong kid. They thought they were kidnapping the Romero boy. They're probably contacting the father right now looking for a ransom." "How about Mr. McKinley, sir?" I ventured.

"You're right. I've got to call him now." The Major' face squiched up like he was eating a lemon, and he mumbled to himself, "Should I call that damn alumni as well?" He shook his head and then turned to me. "See what we have on file for that hillbilly's number." He pointed toward one of four filing cabinets. I rummaged through to the M's and pulled Rob's file. "Mr. McKinley doesn't have a home phone. All we have is a work phone at someplace called the Newton Bottling Plant."

"Well, I might as well bite the bullet." He picked up the receiver of his phone. "Give me the number," he said.

CHAPTER 12
Rob's story continues

I weren't a mile down the gravel road parallelin' the feeder track headin' into Newton, when the thunderhead clouds turned from gray to black and the Lord pulled the cork. The rain began to slap my face. I shoved my head down into my flannel shirt like a turtle into his shell and picked up the pace.

The rain clouds soon blackened the entire sky and a wind came up and blew leaves across the road. Lightnin' zig -zagged, flickered and hissed. I took shelter under the spreadin' branches of a huge oak by the side of the road and waited for the deluge to subside.

After a few minutes, the rain settled down to a drizzle that dimpled the puddles that had formed on the gravel road and I headed out again, not in the least bothered that I was now soaked and shiverin'.

It was a little before three in the afternoon, when I saw the outskirts of Newton and circled carefully around the town to the Newton mansion. I hid behind the big magnolia tree across the path from the mansion and waited for Katie to come home from school.

The afternoon had cooled and the drizzle was several degrees warmer and bland as perfumed bath powder. I could feel my heart beatin' and felt the blood pumpin' in the back of my neck in anticipation of seein' Katie. I breathed deeply through my open mouth.

Katie came peddlin' along on her red Schwinn bicycle. I took a deep breath and stepped from behind the tree. She hit her brakes. She stood straddlin' her bike. Taller and thinner than I remembered. But, still my blond haired angel.

"Robby!"

"Hi, Katie. How ya doin'?" I postured nonchalant like.

Katie looked like she'd seen a ghost. "What are you doing here?" She whispered. I straightened up and looked closely at her. Her checks was a little gaunt and her rosy complexion was sallow. I tossed my head to dislodge a cowlick that wasn't there. "I came to help you."

Katie dropped the bike and ran to me. I roughly put my arms around her and could hear her muffled voice buried in my shirt. "Oh, Robby, I've been so afraid."

My hand drifted softly over her hair like I was fondlin' an heirloom. The rain had stopped and the air was cool and clean and sweet smellin'. It was like a dream.

"It's gonna be alright, Katie."

She stepped back, took both of my shoulders in her hands and looked up at me. "You look so different." She smiled. "You've grown a bunch ... you stand so straight ... and you look so cute in a crewcut."

I took hold of her arm. "Let's get outta sight before somebody sees me."

How did you get out of that academy?"

"I ran away when I got your last letter and hopped a freight. Come on." I tugged her over to her bike. "Put this away and let's go down by the river."

Katie dropped the bike by her porch and put a little skip in her gait as she trotted back. A few minutes later, we was hidden from view in a hammock of bay trees with an undergrowth of thorny bushes next to the river. Katie said, "Why didn't you write me?"

"I must'a wrote you a hundred letters."

"Honest?"

"Honest." I nodded. "Someone's gettin' your mail."

We sat in thoughtful silence for several minutes and then Katie sighed, "Daddy's been grabbing your letters, I guess."

I nodded.

Katie placed the palms of both of her hands on my cheeks, kissed me and leaned back. I nervously opened and closed my hands, wiped them on my trousers, breathed deeply and slowly through my mouth, and firmly returned the kiss. Katie leaned back after a minute. "Won't that academy be looking for you?"

I nodded. "But not here, at least right away. My friend, the Sergeant, is going to cover for me as long as he can. It should give us enough time to get the proof for your daddy that Crafton's going into competition with him."

Katie sat down on a stump and smiled. "I know you've got a plan. What is it?"

We got a mess of things to do, I been thinkin'," I said. "First off, find out who that big guy was who wanted to kill you if you told anybody 'bout him. The second is, what's he goin' to be deliverin' that Crafton needs and finally what's goin' on in that barn."

Katie said, "The answers to all of those start at the barn, but you've been caught both times you went there at night and Crafton was there."

"Crafton and that pilot fella both work there at night after their regular jobs. If we went there right now, the only person that might show up is Billy. I can handle Billy,"

Katie said, "You won't have to. He and the other guys all play baseball after school for a couple of hours."

"Then, I gotta get a move on," I said.

Katie stood up, her face flushed in excitement. "Not without me."

"I don't wanna put you in any danger," I said. "I'll go by myself."

Katie shook her head. "Daddy's not going to believe anything you say you saw. And he certainly isn't going to embarass Mr. Crafton by investigating. He'll just get your dad and they'll send you back to the academy. I've got to go with you to the barn."

I picked up a rock and got a three bounce skip across the river's surface. "Then, let's get to goin'."

Katie was so excited she was almost dancin'. "Mom's expecting me home any minute. She'll call daddy if I'm late. But, I always walk Buffy when I get home from school. Let me run home and get Buffy."

I thought for a minute. "Can you get a screwdriver and maybe a pair of pliers while you're home?"

"Sure. Why?" Katie asked.

"Well, I'm thinkin' the barn door will be locked and I sure didn't have much of a view of the inside of the barn through the crack when the lights was on. I won't see nothin' if there's no light on inside durin' the day."

"So, why the screwdriver?' Katie asked.

"I noticed a little window kind'a high up. We might just be able to get into the barn that way."

Katie clapped her hands. "Wait here. I'll be back in fifteen minutes."

The fifteen minutes turned out to be more like forty and seemed like a hundred. She arrived in a gray blouse, girl's khaki pants and hikin' boots. She had Buffy on a leash and a sack of stuff. I asked, "What're you gonna do with your dog?" Buffy was a little black Lhasa Apso.

"I'll leave her here," Katie proceeded to tie Buffy's leash to a limb of the magnolia tree. "Nobody can see her from here and she obeys me real well. Stay, Buffy." She ordered, "And be quiet!"

Buffy curled up under the tree, but her eyes was totally alert and her ears was stickin' straight up. Katie stroked her head and said, "I'll be back real soon."

Off we went. Crafton's place was between the Newton mansion and Milton's river store. Part of his four or five acres butted up to the river. We followed the path back to where Crafton's property started and then cut through his field the same way I'd gone the night this whole mess got started.

Once we was a few hundred yards from the barn, we looked up to the Crafton house several hundred yards beyond. A single car old garage was a few yards away from the house and an old rusty John Deere tractor was parked up next to the kitchen side of the house between the house and garage. Crafton's pickup was gone and there was no sign of life.

"Come on, Katie!" I squeezed her hand and we ran to the barn. I took a second to look into the crack but it had been plastered shut. I moved to the little window. It weren't quite as high up as I remembered, but still too high for me to reach from the ground. I looked at it closely and saw it was hinged to swing out and the hinges was all exposed.

"Katie," I whispered, "See them hinges?" I pointed up. "Sure," she answered.

"Get on my shoulders and see if you can unscrew 'em." I squatted in front of the window. Katie took a screwdriver and a flashlight outta her bag and dropped the rest in the grass. She got her balance holding onto the side of the barn and climbed onto my shoulders. A couple of minutes later, she handed the screws down to me with her free hand. I put then into a pocket. She then slid the little window slowly down the wall and I grabbed it and dropped it quietly onto the grass. Katie said, "I'm going in."

A second later she squirmed through the openin' and was gone. I heard her muffled voice yell, "Come to the main door."

By the time I got there, she had raised the locking bar and opened the door. We both stood there in stunned silence.

The barn was a full-blown bottling plant; complete with a conveyer belt for the bottles in this case, bottles the same size and shape as the Dr. Pepper bottles but dark green without a label. Adjacent to the conveyer belt was a bunch of five gallon jugs, each with siphon hoses ready to fill the bottles once the belt started. At the end of the conveyer belt, there was a box of caps, a capping machine and beyond that was plywood crates for shippin' Dr. Pepper soda pop.

It was a bottlin' plant all right, but one thing was wrong with the picture; the whole durn barn stunk to high heaven of whiskey!

Katie gasped, "Robby, Crafton's bottling moonshine whiskey!" I put my arm around her shoulder and hugged. "Crafton's not goin' into competition with your dad's plant, he's using the plant's distribution network to sell moonshine from here all the way up to Valdosta!"

"How do you know that?" Katie whispered.

"A guy I met on the train told me he had a hangover from moonshine he'd bought in Valdosta supplied by a soft drink distributor. The bottle I saw on the train was just like these."

Katie said, "Daddy's going to be furious with Crafton." She looked up at me and smiled. "But we've got proof your suspicion was right. Something illegal is going on here."

"Let's get outta here before someone comes along," I said and pointed toward the door. "You go on out and I'll relock up from the inside and climb outta the window."

After I locked the door behind Katie, I did a quick look around the barn to see if there was anything else of interest to be learned about but there wasn't nothin'. So, I climbed up onto a table under the window and picked up the black window shade Katie'd knocked to the table when she climbed in. I squirmed out the window backwards on my belly and put the window shade back in place before droppin' to the ground.

On my feet again, I helped boost Katie back onto my shoulders and handed her up the little window and the screws.

"Oh, shoot!" She said.

"What is it?

I knocked that darn window shade off again trying to put the window in place. We're going to have to go back inside and get it."

"It's gettin' too late for us to be here. Crafton or that pilot can come at any time. Just screw the window hinges back on. They'll probably assume a rat or somethin' else knocked the shade down."

Katie nodded and grunted as she set the wood screws into place, "Besides, I'm going straight home and call daddy. He'll be here with the sheriff in an hour."

A few minutes later, we headed out across the field. Katie said, "We've got to pick up Buffy-Robby, there's Billy Crafton coming down the road."

I spun my head around and sure 'nough Billy was comin' up his driveway. He spotted us at about the same time I seen him. He stood lookin' at us with his hands on his hips for a minute and then went into the house and slammed the door.

"Come on," I said and took Katie's hand. "Let's run over behind their garage where he can't see us from a window."

Katie panted as we stopped behind the garage. "Do you think he's going to call his dad about us?"

"I don't know but sure would like to find out."

"I think we better run to my house," Katie whispered.

"Just a minute," I said. "Crafton's phone is next to the kitchen window. I seen Mr. Crafton call someone from it the night he caught me. Whoever it was told him to let me go."

"Then, Crafton has a boss in this moonshine operation." Katie concluded.

I nodded and then peeked my head around the corner of the building just in time to see Billy pick up the phone and turn his back to the open kitchen window.

"Come on," I whispered to Katie. "let's slip over behind that ol' tractor and see if we can hear anything."

Katie's face was gettin' pretty white but she nodded okay and we ran lightly over to the tractor and squatted down outta sight.

"Pa, it's Billy. I don't know if it's important or not, but I forgot to take my mitt to school and came home just now to pick it up ... okay, I'm sorry, I'll get to the point. I remembered how mad you was when Robby McKinley was sneakin' around our barn last time ... pa, just let me finish. Yes, I just saw Katie Newton with a kid that could have been Robby McKinley walkin' across our field. They might have been comin' from the barn".

Billy turned and looked out the window across the field. "No, I don't see them no more." He stood there noddin' his head for a spell and then said, "I can't be sure it was Rob. They was a way off. The kid was a lot bigger than I remember Robby bein'. and there was somethin' differn't 'bout his hair. So it might not of been him."

Billy started noddin again like he was takin' directions. After a time, he said, "I understand. You're gonna come home now and see what's goin' on. I'm goin' back to school to my baseball game. I'll be home in time for supper."

He hung up the phone, and with mitt in hand slammed out the door.

Katie said, "Let's make a bee-line home."

"I put my hand on her arm and whispered, "Let's wait a few minutes and see what Crafton does when he gets here. He might even bring the guy he called the last time. I'd like to find out who the boss is."

We got settled in real good between the tractor's two big back wheels totally outta sight from anywhere in the house. About ten minutes later, I saw Crafton pull in front of the barn and check the door. He then walked all the way around the barn and was startin' to get back in his pickup when Rusty Yates, the pilot, skidded to a stop in an old Chevy sedan.

They talked for a minute but was too far away for us to

hear anything. They both got into Crafton's pickup and drove up to the house. We heard the two pickup doors slam and Crafton said, "I've gotta let the boss know about this."

Katie squeezed my hand.

Rusty answered, "Couldn't something else have knocked that shade down?"

"Maybe."

They went in the front door around the corner from us and then reappeared in the kitchen window. We scrunched down a bunch more while Crafton was dialin' the phone.

"Doc? Crafton here. I got some bad news. Your daughter's been back snooping around the barn again, I think, along with a kid that could'a been the McKinley boy. No, I didn't see them, but Billy did. They was crossin' my field as if they'd been out at the barn ... no, Billy was clear across the field from them. He's sure it was your daughter though and the boy looked a little like the McKinley boy. No, he couldn't be sure. Un huh, uh huh. My boy called me like he's supposed to ... no, they was gone when I got home ... I understand. You're gonna come right on over ... no, I ain't gonna panic none, we'll figure out what we gotta do. I think findin' them kids is the first priority before they shoot their mouths off to someone. Uh huh, uh huh, I gotcha. No, I'll wait right here until you get here."

We heard the receiver bein' set into place.

Rusty asked, "What'd he say?"

Crafton answered, "He said he'd take care of keepin' his daughter's mouth shut. The important thing is to clear out the barn immediately and then fan out and find that boy. If we don't find him in time and he brings the sheriff to the barn, we'll be okay if there ain't nothin' there to see."

"When we find the boy, how will we shut him up?" Rusty asked.

"For good, that's how!" Crafton said.

Rusty said, "How about Luke?"

Crafton answered, "You're right. You've gotta tell him what's happened on your next pick up. If you don't ." He shuddered." They got in the pickup and drove back toward the barn.

Katie looked at me but didn't say nothin'. Her eyes said it all.

I said, "I'm real sorry, Katie."

Katie whispered, "That big man must be the one called Luke."

I helped her to her feet and we headed out away from the Crafton's with the garage between us and the barn.

"Katie, do you remember the man I told you I met that had a moonshine hangover?"

"Yes, what about him?"

"He told me his brother's name was Luke. But that's probably just a coincidence 'cause his brother's in a maximum security prison down south for life."

Katie stopped in her tracks and grabbed my arm; her fingernails dug into the skin. "A couple of months ago, mom and dad were talking about the news over dinner. Mom said she'd seen on TV that a convicted murderer had escaped from the state prison. She said his name, I've forgotten what it was, and daddy seemed surprised. Daddy said, 'I know that man. I had to sew him up years ago after a knife fight he was in."

I said, "I'll bet it was Smokey's brother."

Katie slumped her shoulders. "I can't go home and face daddy."

I said, "I'll go to town and get the sheriff."

"Robby, if the sheriff sees what's going on in Crafton's barn he'll have to arrest my daddy."

I flayed my jelly like mind ... where was my agile whip-like brain? Katie continued, "And as soon as Crafton and Rusty Yates get the barn cleared out, they'll go to town looking for you. The sheriff is never in his office so you'll have to wait there until he stops in at the end of the day. Crafton will grab you for sure. He said he was going to shut you up for good!"

I said, "Well, how 'bout you? Rusty's gonna tell Luke about you on his next pick-up and Luke has threatened to snap your neck!"

Katie started to cry softly and after a few minutes of walkin' along she said," We can't deal with this alone, Robby. We need adult help."

"I've got a friend who'll help," I said.

"Who?"

"Smokey, Luke's brother. He was real nice to me and helped me get home. He told me he'd be there for me if I needed anything."

"Where is he? Katie asked.

Sunlight through the trees we were now in made a pattern on her bare legs. Buffy saw us and proceeded to bark until Katie untied her and picked her up.

I pointed beyond the river into the swamp. "About fifteen miles due north right through there."

"How'd we get there?"

"In my boat. I've got a map." I reached into my rear pocket, pulled out the paper sack and waved it at her. In the process, my shirt tail popped out. There wasn't a shirt made that could stay in my jeans.

Katie exclaimed, "Let's do it!"

A great blue heron took off from the river and soared overhead with slow flappin' wings.

I skipped a flat rock across the river and said, "We'll need a few things; a compass, matches, some canned goods and a can opener to carry us over on our trip through the swamp. Here," I reached in my pocket, "I've got most of twenty dollars."

Katie smiled, "When I went home earlier for the screwdriver and flashlight, I decided to get my allowance money out of the cigar box I keep it hidden in." She reached into a pocket and showed me a wad of money.

"Why did 'ja do that?"

"I'm sorry, but I thought there was a real good chance we weren't going to see anything wrong at the barn. And if there wasn't, the best thing for you was to take the next bus back to your academy." She shook the wad of money at me. "This was to pay for your trip back."

I smiled and we made a plan. We made up a list of anything we might need in the days ahead. Katie would stay outta sight walkin' over to Milton's store to buy those things and then return to this spot by the river and stay outta sight until I got back with my boat.

It was goin' on ten by the time I got back. Katie was behind a tree with Buffy in her arms. She whispered, "Robby?"

A crescent moon wanly stuck through the clouds and glimmered on the dark blue and turquoise expanse of water as I stepped into view.

"My boat's half sunk. Only the bow is outta the water. It's gonna take me awhile to raise and patch it."

"What took you all this time?"

"Well, for one your daddy's car was in the yard so I stayed outta sight until he left."

"Daddy's looking for you," Katie whispered.

I nodded. "I'll be back as soon as I can."

"Can't I come?"

"Not with your dog. I can't risk wakin' dad."

Twenty minutes later, I peeked into my dad's kitchen. Dad was passed out with his head on the table with a half empty bottle in front of him. It made my stomach ache. I tiptoed on past the shack and undid the hemp rope that tied my sunken boat to a tree.

A low growl came from the shack's front porch. It was Epidus tied to a long rope. She slid off the porch and stealthily moved toward me with the hair on her neck standin' up like a porcupine. She growled again. I gave her a low whistle. She stopped. looked, leaped forward and knocked me on my butt. She smothered me in dog kisses. I kept my laughter in my head and whispered,

"Don't wake dad," as I untied her.

It was nearly daylight when I poled up to the meetin'

spot with Epidus standin' in the bow of the boat like Washington crossin' the Delaware. She leaped out and barked at Katie huddled under a tree.

Buffy scrambled out of Katie's arms and raced forward to defend her mistress. I jumped out of the boat and grabbed Epidus by the collar.

"Ep' if you're gonna come with us, you'd better get to be friends with Miss Buffy, here."

Buffy growled in disgust and turned back to Katie.

Katie stood shiverin' with her arms crossin' her chest. She whispered, "I thought you'd never come."

I shrugged and smiled.

She grimaced at the peelin', faded blue flat-bottom boat.

I said, "It took some doing but I think we've got a water tight boat." I looked into her face. "Come and get on board. I'd like to be on our way before it gets any lighter." Katie wrinkled up her nose at the smell of pitch and stepped into my boat as tentative as a bird.

CHAPTER 13

Marvin's story continued:

Mr. McKinley pulled in the next morning just as I was calling my troops into formation. He must have driven through the night. His truck skidded to a halt in a cloud of dust in front of the Major's office and he hopped out. Just like the first time I saw him, he was dressed in overalls and it looked like he probably hadn't shaved in two or three days.

I'd been having a lot of second thoughts about leading the Major into thinking Rob had been kidnapped. Now, I really felt a huge chest pang of guilt seeing the fear and concern in Mr. McKinley's eyes. I marched the troops to the Mess and then sauntered back across to the Infirmary where I could keep an eye on the Major's office.

After a few minutes, they came out together and walked rapidly across to R Company barracks. I figured they were going to Rob's room and scooted behind the barracks pretty much out of sight and got as close to Rob's window as I could and still not be seen.

"So, you'all are tellin' me that my boy has been kidnapped by a gang of Cuban thugs?" I could hear Mr. McKinley through the open window.

"That's my theory, Mr. McKinley. You see, I didn't know it, but your boy's roommate is the son of a well known Cuban gangster. Part of dictator Batista's crowd that this young fella, Castro, sent packing after his revolution last year. Probably has lots of enemies."

"And that boy's in the hospital?"

"Yes sir, but the kidnappers would have no way of knowing it. My speculation is that somebody who works for, or is very close to, Romero planned it. Somebody who could have had access to his mail. Probably grabbed one of Rudy Romero's letters to his dad and found out where he was in fact, even his room and barrack's number. When they slipped into his room three nights ago, they had no reason to suspect they were getting the wrong boy. As you can see, Romero's bunk bedding had been removed and the mattress rolled up military fashion. It would have been obvious only one boy lived here." The Major pointed toward Rob's bunk. "So, they had to assume they had the right kid."

"Well they sure as hell wouldn't think my boy was Cuban in the light'a day."

"Cubans come in all colors. Some are as white as you and I."

"Rob would have told them who he was."

"I know. That's a bit of a problem, but the Savannah Police theorize that even if the kidnappers had their doubts, they were just flunkies following orders and would follow through with a ransom demand to the father."

Mr. McKinley's voice boomed out the window. "Well, has the Cuban got one?"

"The Savannah police have asked assistance from their counterparts in Miami. The last I heard is Miami hasn't had any luck contacting Romero. They think he might be in Cuba."

"Why'd you wait so long to call me?"

"Well, I thought he'd simply run away from the Fort."

"Why'd you think he'd do that? My boy don't run away from nothin'."

"To be frank, Mr. McKinley, your boy was ill-suited for the Academy. He simply didn't fit in. Couldn't get along with the other cadets, was rebellious and insubordinate. I was about to write you a letter to tell you I was going to have to expel him."

"Rob's a good boy and he didn't tell me nothin' about those kind'a problems in his letters." Mr. McKinley's voice got louder by a whole bunch of decibels.

"You can believe me, Mr. McKinley. I'm sorry to have to tell you, but your son just isn't Fort material." The Major postured and continued. "You can ask his Squad Sergeant, Marvin Ellis. Ellis really tried his best with him. We knew he wasn't exactly on the same playing field, should I say, with the other boys; most of our cadets are second or third generation here at the Fort. Ellis and I went out of our way to make your son feel welcome and to get him over some of his arrogant and primative behavior. I frankly have never tried so hard with any other boy."

When I heard this baloney, I was so put out I scooted closer to the window and could see their reflections in the wall mirror. Mr. McKinley's face looked like one of the Mt. Rushmore president's carved in granite. He said in measured tones, "What can I do to help find my boy?"

"Just go on home. Stay out of our way. We'll get in touch as soon as we find him."

"Don't the police have no clues? In three days nobody a'tall seen nothin'?"

"Just his fatigues. Now go on home, Mr. McKinley and leave this to professionals. I'll send for you to pick him up as soon as we have him."

They moved out the door and I made a bee-line for the front gate on a high run. I was down in front of the Mom and

106

Pop out of breath and winded when I saw the rusty old pickup heading toward me down the road. I waved it down.

CHAPTER 14
Rob's Story Continued:

Once we crossed the river, I pulled out Smokey's map and studied it. "We wanna enter that channel right over there next to that grove of longleaf pines."

I stood in the rear of the boat and pushed a long wooden pole to the bottom of the stagnant river, shallow at this point. I shoved the boat forward toward a protected cocoon of wooded wetlands with islands covered with palms, sweet bay, and a vast expanse of brown needle rush and saw grass.

Katie sat facin' me on a boat cross member near the front strokin' Buffy in her lap. Epidus had claimed the forward observer position and was leadin' the way with a waggin' tail. By late mornin', we was polin' through a blue smear of water under overhangin' banks. It was as silent as a mausoleum except for the occasional swift slur of approachin' ducks or the chirpin' of a blue jay preenin' her feathers.

Katie asked me, "Would you like to take a break from that poling and have some lunch?"

"What'cha got? I'm so hungry I could eat a folded tarp."

"Fixings for a tuna sandwich."

I smiled and poled toward a point of land a foot out of the water a few square yards in diameter and pretty dry. I pulled a waterproof tarp out from under the bow, unzipped it and removed my .410 shotgun and fishin' gear. I put the gun and fishin' gear back under the bow, stuffed the tarp under my arm and hopped out onto a bank of black muck smellin' of decay. Katie joined me and felt the muck suckin' at her boots.

We climbed out of the muck onto a clean carpet of pine needles and brittle oak leaves blown over from the shore and spread the tarp. While Katie prepared the sandwiches, I pointed out a family of long-tusked wild boars strollin' through wild plums and mangos on the shore.

"There'll be food aplenty, Katie."

"Hogs and plums?" A shaft of sunlight cut across her wrinkled nose.

I laughed, "In the last hour, I've spotted wild mustard greens, swamp cabbage and a bunch of turtles. Where there's turtles, there's turtle eggs for eatin'."

Katie offered a cheerful smile. "I'm sure we'll do just fine."

She fed the last part of her sandwich to Buffy.

I stood up. "Looks like we're in for some rain again this afternoon." I handed the last of my sandwich to Epidus. "Let's get goin'."

"Okay, but it's my turn to pole," Katie said.

I didn't point out the black heads of water moccasins I saw stickin' out of the water like motionless twigs a few yards from our island. There was no breath of coolness anywhere.

Cloud piled on cloud and the atmosphere became stiflin'. An hour later, a violent cloud burst struck us with tropical fury in heavy gray curtains. We could hear palm leaves swishin' on shore. Katie pulled the pole into the boat and the four of us sought shelter under the tarp until the cloudburst stopped as quickly as it had started.

Afterwards, the air was cooled and the world was a sparklin' mass of rain drops on green leaves and a chorus of frogs and crickets.

Katie handed the pole to me with a cheerless smile. We took turns at the pole and consultin' the map until evenin'. We fell into exhausted silence. "I'm going to pull under that tree for the night, Katie, I'm a mite tuckered." I grunted and poled under an upturned cypress stump that was nearly petrified.

Minutes later, we was ashore and had started a fire with fatwood chips and oak twigs. I saw familiar traces where a turtle had dug, laid her eggs, and then packed the sand with her back flippers. We was soon boilin' turtle eggs the size of golf balls in the deep skillet Katie had brought.

An evenin' breeze out of the bayou kicked up and kindly pushed swarms of mosquitos back into the trees so the four of us could eat in peace.

A last wash of sunset ran zigzaggin' through the woods, layin' fiery red lingerin' fingers across the trees as I studied Smokey's map.

"We're right on course." I refolded the sack and said with a wistful and tired grin, "We're at least halfway to Smokey's."

"Let's sleep on the boat, Robby," Katie said, as she washed the skillet in water made cloudy green from the earlier rain. "Being on shore jangles my nerves with all the snakes and stuff."

The idea of sleepin' with Katie was enough to stoke the coals of my furnace. I'd been thinkin' about it all day.

"Robby, I've got to go the toilet before we bed down. Would you get in the boat and turn your head." Katie smiled in an embarrassed way.

"Sure, I don't mind." As tired as I was, I still felt a warm glow.

A few minutes later, Katie took my hand and climbed into the boat. She glanced at my flushed face.

"Robby."

"Yes, Katie."

"We better talk."

"'Bout what?"

"About us."

"What about us?"

"You know."

"Oh."

"There's nothing we can do."

I blushed from ear to ear and said, "I don't know what you're talkin' 'bout."

I spread the tarp over the bottom of the boat for something to do and then grabbed Ep' and cuddled her up close on one side of the boat.

"Robby, are you upset?"

"No, of course not."

The woods was alive with rustlin' critters gettin' ready for the night. Some creatures on their way to bed, others awakenin' from the day's sleep.

"Goodnight, Katie."

I looked up at the stars for a few minutes while I settled down. I must have been pretty tired because I was soon lured to sleep by a frog Philharmonic. Katie awakened once durin' the night to the peculiar cry of a bull 'gator callin' his mate. There was no breeze and the water was still and black and dented in the moon's reflection. She scooted closer into my back and went back to sleep, as peaceful as a thumb in a baby's mouth. I had a hard time gettin' back to sleep after that, let me tell you.

Greeted at sunrise by a singin' mockingbird we rubbed our eyes and sat up. Somethin' was wrong. There was no stump in sight and no clear channel water. The boat was surrounded by tall grass and there was an odor of dead fish and sour mud. Except for the mockingbird, it was as scene as a prayer meetin'.

"We've drifted durin' the night," I gasped.

"Great guns! Where to?"

I stood on my toes on the cross member and looked one way and then another but couldn't seem to decide. "I can't see a thing." I stepped down. "I don't know."
"It looks like we got caught up in this grass." My eyes squeezed shut for a few agonizin' seconds. "Reckon we're lost."
Katie squeezed my hand. "We'll figure out something." She looked down at a leaf slowly driftin' past. "We drifted from that direction." She pointed into the grass-she has a sensitive antenna. We've got to get back where we were last night to get our bearings."

"I'll push us back the way we came." I grabbed the pole. Epidus resumed her navigator position and Katie tried to figure out where we might be on the map. Buffy went back to sleep.

I pushed and strained for an hour. The goin' was slow. It was as if the channel we'd been on had dissolved suddenly into a spread of flat confusion covered in tall river grass, brittle and gold interspersed with butter-yellow flowers.

The marsh had closed in over the channel we'd come on. We was in a maze. Katie took her turn at the pole but the resistance of the grass was too much for her small arms. By noon, my mouth was as dry as old popcorn and I was losin' my confidence.

I said, "I reckon I can't be sure I'm not just pushin' us around in circles, and that's a fact."

Katie was still studyin' the map. Suddenly her hand flew to her mouth and she let out a "whoop" like a war cry, "The compass!"

She grabbed her knapp sack, threw the skillet aside and dug. "We'll just push north and we'll find the channel again." She pulled the compass out triumphantly and pointed. "Pole that way, Robby."

I felt so dumb I couldn't teach a chicken how to cluck. I struggled for another hour but it was clear I weren't makin' much headway.

"Rest a bit, Robby."

I laid down the pole and crashed onto the cross member beside Katie. After a few shallow breathes, I said, "I'm not makin' it pushin'. Reckon I'm gonna have to pull."

Katie gasped, "Get in that filthy water full of water moccasins and alligators? No, Robby!"

"Got no choice." I slowly stood up and stretched. "We're not goin' anywhere the way it is." I picked up the tie-down rope connected to a metal hoop in the center of the bow of the boat and slid myself slowly over the side. I didn't let on but my body was covered in goose bumps. "I got you into this. I'll get you out." I was as cross as a snappin' turtle.

The stink hit me as I slid into the murky water. It was rotten and acrid and sweet at the same time. Reekin' of salt and decay, fetid and gray as a rat's breath. I gagged and held my fist to my mouth. I swallowed back a taste of vomit, put the rope over one shoulder and waded forward.

The black water was over my waist. Katie looked on in horror, so I turned and gave a confident grin. "Keep pointin' me north."

Epidus was beside herself jumpin' around the boat barkin' at me.

"Quiet, Ep'," I ordered. "Stay."

Buffy, sittin' in Katie's lap, looked at me apprehensively.

By late afternoon, I guessed we'd covered a mile or more and we was mostly out of the tall grass but couldn't recognize nothin' that looked like our map. Channels extended out in multiple directions ; some shallow with no outlets, others broad as a stream.

The marsh and water glittered in the sun. Solid land made its way here and there. We saw several alligators sunnin' themselves on the bank. Our universe was a yellow marsh with lakes linked together. I kept pullin' in the direction Katie pointed.

At dusk I climbed, well drug, myself aboard. Katie had prepared me the last of the tuna as a sandwich, but I was too tired to eat and dropped my head into her lap, oblivious to the swarms of mosquitos settlin' in like a gray cloud lookin' for exposed flesh. I felt so sick, I'd of had to get better to die.

Katie covered all of us with the tarp careful not to disturb me. My stomach was rumblin'. Mom used to joke that if I missed a meal my gut would soon announce it like an anvil.

Katie dozed fitfully in a sittin' position 'til the sun came up soft and pink in a mist that rose from the trees across the bayou. After a time, I struggled awake and shared a few bites of the final stale tuna sandwich with Katie, Buffy and Epidus.

Katie's face had half a dozen mosquito bites. Her hair looked sweaty and dirty. Her eyes was red-rimmed. That's when I realized she'd stayed awake while I was sleeping in her lap. I had to hug her. "It'll be okay," I said.

My shoulders shuddered involuntarily as I slid back into the murky water and grabbed the rope and stepped forward. Katie's tired eyes crossed as she tried to keep them focused on the compass held in one hand. She had Buffy's collar grasped in the other. Buffy was sick of the boat and was growlin' irritably at Epidus.

All of a sudden, in mid-morning, Katie screamed. Epidus spun about, looked out and saw a water moccasin swimmin' from the side toward me. Its shiny black head was stickin' inches above the water's surface as its body wiggled rapidly through the green water. Epidus poised to jump over the side.

I looked over my shoulder at the commotion and yelled, "Stay Ep'!"

Katie dropped Buffy and grabbed the pole as the poison-ous snake closed the last few feet to me. I dropped the rope and didn't even know it. Katie held the pole like a long ax and slammed it down and splashed water everywhere. The snake just kept swimmin' along right on past me like nothin' had happened.

"I think you scared him off, Katie," I croaked. "Thanks."

Katie sat back down and grimaced at me. I turned back to pullin', but now I constantly scanned the water's surface.

Within minutes, a total weakness swept over me. I stopped and swayed for a moment lookin' into the sky. A thousand little star spots swam before my eyes. I thought I was gonna faint. I forced my eyes down to the horizon and felt a little better.

Katie yelled to me, "What is it?"

I slowly turned around and pulled the boat to me.

"I feel bad, Katie." I slumped against the boat, suddenly shakin' like I'd dropped onto the North Pole. "I'm gonna pull us over to shore and start a fire."

I tied the boat to a small cypress tree and gathered pine needles to start a fire. Katie looked across the marsh at sunnin' alligators.

"I'm going to boil us up some drinking water, Robby. You take a rest."

I dropped to the grass, stretched, and passed out. Both Epidus and Buffy cuddled up tight against my back and was soon asleep.

"Reckon you're lost."

Katie felt a hand on her shoulder and jumped nearly out of her skin. The man was big with black eyes sunken in fleshy folds. He had a juttin' slab of a jaw and grisly iron-gray whiskers and hair. One muddy, baggy trouser leg was rolled up halfway to his calf.

Epidus leaped to her feet and uttered a deep growl.

Katie gasped, her voice worn down to a whisper. "Where'd you come from?"

I noticed the man's resemblence to Smokey.

CHAPTER 15

Marvin's Story Continued:

Mr. McKinley pulled off the asphalt and threw up a cloud of red Geogia dust in front of the Mom and Pop. I was waiting by his driver's side window by the time he got the glass rolled down.

"Hi, Mr. McKinley, do you remember me?" I asked.

He nodded his head, his face like a mask. "Sergeant Marvin Ellis."

"Yes sir, you got a minute to talk with me about Rob?"

He jerked his head toward my side of the cab. "Hop in."

I jumped in and slammed the door.

He said, "Go on and talk."

"I heard some of what the Major told you. And, it isn't quite right." I stammered.and paused.

"Tell it like it is, boy."

So, I did. Right from the start. How the Major ordered me to make Rob's life a living hell. I described all the hazing I'd done to Rob and Rudy.

"Get to the point," he said.

"Rob hasn't been kidnapped," I said. "He had to get out

of here. He was a good cadet, but the Major was out to get him."

"Why?"

I looked toward the window. "He called Rob, 'the son of a drunken Florida Cracker'."

A flush started climbing right up his neck. "Sounds like you was out to get him too. Why'd ya change your mind?" He looked at me like I was some kind of vermin.

"Because Rob and Rudy saved my life."

The flush waned and I saw his eyes dampen as I told him the story without sparing myself. After I was finished, we sat quietly for a minute. Then, Mr. McKinley wiped the back of his hand across his forehead and asked, "Do you know where I can find him?"

"The last I saw him," I answered, "I'd pushed him aboard a freight down by the Interstate bound for Valdosta. All he had was the clothes on he'd arrived here in and a twenty dollar bill I gave him."

Mr. McKinley twisted the truck key, started the engine and nodded at my door. "After I find my boy, I guess I'd better come back here and have a chaw with that soldier boy of yours."

I shuddered for the Major's sake.

CHAPTER 16

Rob's Story Continued:

"I live t'other side of the creek." The man pulled a large revolver from his waist band and pointed it at Epidus. "Saw your smoke. What're you kids doing out here among the varmints?"

Epidus' growl brought me to my feet.

Katie chirped with an uncertain voice, "Robby, we've got a visitor."

Epidus sensed terrible danger and inched toward the stranger; her growl grew more ferocious.

"That hound move another inch and I'ma going to blow her ugly head off." The man squinted from a dusty sweaty face dotted with liver spots like a map of some foreign country.

"Stay, Ep'!" I yelled, "Don't shoot my dog, mister! She's not gonna move unless I tell her."

"Shaddup. Don't smart mouth me, boy." His mouth was chewed and ravaged by lifelong doubt and suspicion.

My face was flushed and my heart was thumpin'. I gripped my hands together behind my back to hide how scared I was. "I'm sorry." I pulled Epidus back by her collar.

"That's better." The man stuffed the barrel of the revolver back into his waistband. I could see canny deliberation takin' place behind his deadly black eyes.

"I know you, don't I? He said to Katie.

Katie was as white and still as a frightened snow rabbit.

"You're the doctor's girl." The man smirked. " Got yourselves lost out here in the swamp, ain't cha? I thought God took care'a fools and children."

He looked the twin to Smokey in a strange way. Where Smokey was like a friendly middle-aged kid, his brother just looked evil.

"We're not lost," I said. "We're gonna meet a man named Smokey. He taught me how to get around in here."

The man gasped like he'd been stomach punched.

"Mordecai? You know Mordecai?"

"He's a friend of mine."

"Pshaw, he ain't no friend of mine." The man squinted at me.

"You're his brother, ain't cha?"

Katie shot a look of poison arrows at me and I realized my mouth was back in operation again before my brain had kicked in.

"Don't fool with me, boy." Luke grimaced tough as beef jerky.

His name, Luke, didn't exactly tally with that name in the Bible. He moved with the grace of quick silver and Seminole silence to Katie. "I almost snapped your spine." He lightly wiped a dirty palm across Katie's neck.

"Get your hands off of her." I suddenly weren't so afraid and felt my eyes squint down.

"Why, I think not." Luke's eyes grew large and mocked me. "I'm fix'en to take both of you home. You're gonna help me catch-up on my 'shine makin'.

"You're a sinful man," Katie whispered.

Luke laughed, "Sinful? Me sinful? All I do is make a

little 'shine that makes people feel good. It's people like your pappy what's sinful. Only in it for the money. He'd be shocked to find out he's in partnership with me. He probably thinks I'm still livin' in the barred-window ree-sort." He stopped and glared at Katie. "You'all didn't tell him 'bout seein' me. did ya?"

Katie shook her head. Luke laughed again. "You're a smart one, alright." His face got real mean. "Now here's how it's gonna be. I need to cook up as much 'shine as quick as I can for a delivery comin' up in a few days. I'm hurtin' for the money it'll bring. I need hands to help me. You two are goin' to be those hands."

"I'm not going to help you," Katie said.

"You dadgum shore are," Luke said and slapped Katie across the face. I ran forward and swung my best punch into Luke's ample but hard-stomach. Up close, I could smell him. My punch bounced off'n his belly like a tennis ball off a clay court. Luke back-handed me to the ground and Epidus leaped forward and dug her teeth into his ankle.

Luke grabbed at his waistband and pulled out his revolver. I yelled, "Run for it, Ep'!"

Ep' looked at me wild-eye'd and then sprang for the trees. Luke spread his legs and took the revolver in both hands in front of him and sighted down on Ep'. I jumped up and swung on his arms as he fired. He missed Ep' and she was gone. Luke shook me off and back-handed me again up 'side my head.

CHAPTER 17
Dr. Newton's Story Continued:

When I got to Crafton's, he and that squirt , Rusty Yates, had pretty much emptied out the barn. I told them to move the stuff straight away up to Crafton's garage and lock it up and as soon as they were done they were to fan out and find the boy and hold him until I got back. Crafton said he knew what to do with him and I screamed at him, "You don't touch that boy, Joe, and that's an order. Just call me and hold him safe and sound and call me. Our whole business is going down the toilet if this isn't handled right."

Crafton said, "We can't have him goin' to the sheriff, we'll all end up behind bars."

I shook my head, "Listen, Joe, you convinced me to go into this damn supplimental moonshine business just long enough to add the revenue we need to keep the bottling plant going. A few months at best, you said, until the plant is operating in the black on its own. We have twenty employees we've got to keep on the payroll. If we lay them off, their families hell, more than eighty people will go hungry. You know how close that came to happening when I had to shut down the paper factory."

Crafton shook his head and mumbled, "That boy is just too damn nosey."

"You can't hurt that boy, Joe, and that's an order!"

"You're the boss, doctor. But, if we get found out, you'll be in the most trouble. You own the operation. We gotta stop him from talkin'."

I glared. "Oh, and how about my girl?"

"I figure you can keep her quiet since it's all in the family. She won't be wantin' her pappy sent off behind bars."

I did a little deep breathing to calm myself. I felt my world was crashing down around me. "We've got to keep level heads, Joe. This whole moonshine distribution idea was a bad one from the beginning. If I hadn't been so damn desperate for the people of Newton, I never would have agreed to it for even a few months. It's time to shut it down."

Crafton started to argue and I waved my hand in his face and continued. "I'm going home now and tell my girl exactly why we set up this business in the first place. That it was for the survival of the town and all our friends. I'm going to tell her the whole truth; how we felt it was the town's last chance. She's old enough to understand that. I'm also going to tell her we're shutting it down now. That we know it was a mistake. But if she tells anybody about it, several of us will be arrested and I'll lose the Dr. Pepper bottling franchise which will close down this town for sure."

I figeted with the car keys in my pocket and watched Crafton's reaction. After a time, he said, "I reckon your daughter will stay in line. But how 'bout the boy?"

"Your son wasn't even sure it was Robby. But, when you catch him, if it is Robby, I'll bring him home and ask his dad, Ed, to join us. Robby's not stupid. He's not going to want his father out of work." I shook my head. "No, this will work. If Robby has any doubts, I'll have Katie explain how she feels. He's crazy about my girl and will do anything she says."

"What if it's not the McKinley boy?"

"Then he's a transient and nobody is going to take his word over ours-you'll just drive him out to the main highway heading north and south and drop him off."

Crafton lit up a cigarette and slowly nodded. "That's a right good plan. The key now is to find the boy."

I drove home and was so nervous about seeing my Katie, I had to pull over and vomit along the side of the road.

I slammed into the house and bumped into my wife standing behind the door wringing her hands. "Where's Katie?" I asked.

"She's not home yet from walking Buffy. I was praying you'd get here soon. I'm worried. She never stays out on their walks this late. And look what I found."

"Oh, God," I moaned. My wife handed me Katie's empty allowance money cigar box.

I jumped into the Buick and headed out to Ed McKinley's place and pulled into his driveway about eight. The German Shephard barked through the screen door upon my arrival and Ed stumbled out onto the porch. "Good evening, doctor. What can I do for you?" He looked like he already had a snootful.

"Good evening, Ed. Is Robby back home?"

"Why no, Dr. Newton. Why do you ask?"

"Oh, it's nothing important," I lied, "I just thought I saw a boy that looked a little like him on my way home. I wanted to make sure there was nothing wrong at the academy."

"If my boy was here, I'd know 'bout it."

After another twenty minutes of small talk so it wouldn't look like I was as upset as I was, I said goodnight. I drove around the back roads until I realized it was hopeless to find the kids in the dark. When I pulled into my driveway, I found Crafton's pickup waiting.

"Did you find the boy?" I stuck my head out the Buick window.

"Shore didn't. He ain't been to the sheriff yet though. I've got Rusty waiting in the shadows outside Gate's house in case the boy shows up durin' the night. How 'bout your girl?"

I sighed, "I'm afraid she's with the boy."

"What'll we do?"

"Keep Rusty right where he is. Tell him to move close to the sheriff's office in the morning, but stay out of sight. He's to intercept the boy if he shows up and take him back to your place and wait for you to return. Meanwhile, you run over and check out the Greyhound station in Clancy at daylight." That was because Newton was too small to have its own bus station. "The kids have some money and might be just running for it."

"Isn't the McKinley boy supposed to be in some academy up north?"

"He is. I'll call the man in charge as soon as the place opens in the morning. At least we'll be able to find out if the boy is Robby. If this kid with Katie isn't Robby, then we're in luck. He has to be a transient and we can discredit anything he says once I have Katie under control."

In the morning, I called the Officer-in-Charge at Fort Pulaski, a Major Swagart, who assured me no cadets were missing. I swung by the school at recess and looked over the kids on the off chance Katie might have shown up for class, but of course she hadn't. I didn't know where else to look. In the early afternoon, I stopped at Milton's for a cup of coffee and for the heck of it asked the proprietor, Mr. Milton, if my daughter'd been
in the last day or so.

"Why she sure has, doc. I guess you'all are goin' campin'."

"Why do you say that?" I asked.

Ray looked at me a little strange. "Because of what she bought about eight o'clock last night; a skillet, can opener, matches and some canned goods."

"Oh, yeah," I said. "Thanks for the coffee."

Once back in my car, I bit the bullet. It was time to call in Ned Gates, the sheriff, and report Katie missing. I drove straight home and called him. His wife told me he wasn't due home from Valdosta until quite late. She would have him call me first thing in the morning.

CHAPTER 18
Rob's Story Continued:

When my lights came back on, I looked up from lyin' in the bottom of my boat and saw Katie with Buffy in her arms, sittin' on the cross rail of my boat. She was as white as if she'd buried her face in a bowl of flour. Luke was in the back polin' us along. I climbed up and sat besides Katie with my hands holdin' my achin' head. Nobody said nothin'.

Luke tied up to a little rickety wooden dock and ordered us out of the boat. I stepped out onto a blanket of pine needles and looked around. There was a light trail of smoke driftin' above the trees. Luke pushed aside a gray curtain of Spanish moss that was hangin' from the pine tree we was standin' under.

In front of us was a small colorless cypress cabin. I noted that the smoke I'd seen was not comin' from the cabin's chimney but from behind the cabin and out of sight. We walked across the hard red clay that was Luke's front yard and stepped up onto a pine-floored porch. It protested our weight with a groan.

Luke pulled down the latch on the cypress door and

pushed us inside. It was dark 'cept for thin streams of light that shot through the moss-covered shingled roof in a dozen places. It didn't look like the windows had ever been washed. I squinted down my eyes and let them adjust to the dim interior. The room smelled of Luke's unwashed body, rancid salt pork and sour tobacco juice. There was a table with a melted down candle and flies coverin' a saucer of preserved figs. Two cowhide bottomed chairs stood in front of a cold clay fireplace and the gray un-painted walls was covered in dryin' animal skins. A two-burner wood stove was next to the fireplace and I could see a couple of dead catfish floatin' in a bucket of water beside the stove.

A doorless openin' led into a small windowless room that contained a single double bed in serious need of new springs. It dipped in the middle nearly to the floor and the quilt, carelessly yanked across it, was so dirty all trace of its once lively colors was gone. The stench of Luke and whiskey drifted into the room we was in. I saw what I figured was last night's jug layin' on its side with a puddle gettin' soaked up by the unswept floor.

Luke retrieved the jug and took a swig outta what had been spared pourin' out durin' the night because of the shape of the jug. After a minute, he flopped into one of the chairs.

"Well, little lady," he started, "I s'pose you can cook a bit?"

Katie didn't say nothin'.

Luke glared at her a bit. "You'all better speak right up whenever I talk at 'cha."

I said, "She can and so can I."

"That bein' the case," Luke said, "hustle us up some sup-per. We're gonna have a busy day tomorrow." He pointed to-ward the stove. "Thar's a couple of fine catfish I pulled out this mornin'."

I was afraid Katie was gonna say somethin' else that would set Luke off so I took her by the elbow and walked over to the stove. An hour later, we'd prepared well, if the truth be known,

I'd prepared fried catfish and hushpuppies. Katie was like a robot just doin' what I pointed out for her to do. Buffy was right underfoot the entire time with us 'bout to step on her. She wanted nothin' at all to do with Luke.

I was takin' little looks at Luke outta the corner of my eye and seen he was gettin' stoned outta his gourd. I was really scared he was gonna take some kind'a advantage of Katie and was stewin' 'bout how I could stop it.

We ate in total silence. Well, I ate. Katie just sat there lookin' at her plate. Luke, with manners no where near as good as a field hand, gobbled up one entire catfish and most of the hushpuppies hardly without missin' a beat guzzlin' outta his jug. Just as I was slippin' the last hushpuppie under the table to Buffy, Katie up and puked down the front of her blouse.

Luke swayed to his feet and grabbed her by the arm and yanked her across the room. Buffy started to bark and I grabbed her up and ran after them. Luke dragged Katie across a side yard past a big copper drum with a fire burnin' out under it. A copper coil came outta the top and wound around down to a second container. Steam was spewin' out of several poor plumbin' fittin's round the drum. A water-clear liquid dripped into the second container as slowly as turpintine sap. A pile of logs and kindlin' was sittin' beside the drum.

It was Luke's still for makin' moonshine whiskey. Eloise had told me enough about makin' 'shine that I knew the drippin' liquid was the liquid distillate and the big copper drum with the fire under it contained a mixture of mash and water being cooked. The still was sittin' on the bank of a channel and next to a smokehouse. There was no other buildin's.

Luke stopped in front of the smokehouse and waved for me to get up close. He pulled down on a latch and jerked on the smokehouse door. It sorta broke loose all at once like it was rusted shut and hadn't been open in a 'Coon's age. It squeeked open real loud like a rabbit does if you try to grab it. He shoved Katie inside, grabbed me by an arm and slung me into the room and pushed the door shut.

The room was black as a well digger's bottom and smelled of rat droppin's and stagnant damp air. We could faintly hear Luke addin' kindlin' to the fire for a few minutes and then there was total silence. I felt around until I identified the door. There wasn't no inside latch. We might as well of been inside a bank vault.

"Katie."

"Yes."

"We might be here for a spell."

"I know that, Robby. Luke's escaped from prison and desperately needs money."

I put my arm around her shoulder. "He won't be lettin' us go."

"He's paranoid about getting caught and going back to prison." Katie shuddered. "At Mr. Crafton's, he was ready to break my neck and bury me in the swamp just because I'd seen him. He'll kill us before he lets us go."

I hugged her tight. "He ain't gonna hurt us as long as he needs our help."

Katie whispered, "When he thinks he doesn't need us anymore he's going to kill us. We've got to try to escape him even though we haven't a chance."

"We've got a chance."

Katie stiffened up. "What is it?"

I was embarassed to say but knew I had to. "You know my pa has taken to drinkin' the evenin' away."

"I told you I knew."

"Well, lemme tell ya what it's like. The more he drinks the more he wants to talk to someone-me. As long as I was there, he'd bend my ear until he crashed and burned. After that a Cottonmouth could have taken up residence in his bed and he wouldn't 'a stirred."

Katie said, "It looks like Luke is a big drinker."

"Bigger'n my pa, I'd say. I bet he crashes every night."

Katie hunched over. "Even if he does, he's going to lock us up in here at night."

I hugged her tight again. "I'll get him to talkin' like pa. If I can keep him talkin' 'till he's snockered, he might forget 'bout lockin' us up tomorrow."

"And if he doesn't forget?"

"Then maybe the next night," I paused, but realized there was somethin' else that really needed sayin'. "Katie, I'm real concerned Luke might get some unhealthy intentions 'bout you." I squeezed her extra tight when I felt her shudder. I kept talkin', "From now on, keep me 'tween you and Luke. If it looks like he's comin' for you, run like a jackrabbit for the woods and I'll stop him best I can." I felt her nod her head. "We better get some sleep."

CHAPTER 19
Dr. Newton's Story Continued:

The sheriff was at my house at the crack of dawn. I briefed him and then made a quick run to my office to see if Katie'd called me there. I didn't want anybody except the sheriff to know Katie was missing-not quite yet. I returned home just as the Sheriff walked in from our pasture land. "See any sign of her, Ned?" I asked.

"No, shore didn't." He leaned up against his Black and White. "Where do you think she might be headin', Doc?"

I sighed, "Maybe to visit the McKinley boy. I think you know he's up in Savannah."

"Shore. Why would she run off to Savannah and not tell you?"

I blushed. "Because, she's been very concerned about not getting any mail from him since he went into the Academy."

"Should she of?"

I couldn't hide from it. "I been intercepting his letters. I thought it best to nip their little romance in the bud before it got out of hand."

Ned slowly nodded. "So you think she's makin' tracks to find him. You know, young folks can be quite resourceful. Maybe her new friend is the McKinley boy."

I shook my head. "I talked with his dad, Ed McKinley, last night. He assured me he hasn't seen Robby since he left."

Ned nodded again. "Okay. We gotta get a plan goin'."

I just nodded agreement. Ned was going to drive over to Clancy and Smithtown and ask if anybody'd seen Katie. I was going to check with the Newton shop people. By mid-afternoon, I was panicked. My little girl had been out two nights with a strange boy and I couldn't bear the thought of her being out another. I decided she must have learned about my involvement in the moonshine business. Otherwise, she would never have taken off without at least leaving me a note. She was just too thoughtful a girl to let me worry like this. Ned told me we should call a town meeting and break the news that Katie was gone and I agreed.

When the meeting assembled that evening, I asked the community to help find her. Ned told them he believed Katie was trying to get to Savannah by staying off the main roads and camping out. Mr. Francisco observed that we were lucky being situated like we were with a near inpenetrable swamp covering everything to the north. We only had to look in the three other directions.

CHAPTER 20
Rob's Story Continued:

Luke didn't come back that night. When he shoved down the latch in the mornin', bright daylight streamed in and blinded our eyes for a bit. "You'all come on outta thar," he said and kicked at Buffy to keep her in the smokehouse. He was hung over worse'n I ever seen my dad.

He put me and Katie to work scrubbin' out five gallon glass jugs, then heatin' water to a boil and pourin' it into one jug at a time and swishin' it around. Luke was busy fillin' the tank a little at a time with a bucket. He'd walk down to the river to fill the bucket. When he wasn't doin' that, he was stokin' the fire or fillin' one of the now clean and sterilized jugs with moonshine. 'Bout mid-mornin', he put me to choppin' up kindlin' while he stopped to have an occasional 'hair of the dog. I could plainly see he was startin' to feel better.

I said, "Looks to me like there are a bunch of leaks in the system limitin' how much moonshine we can make in a day."

He frowned at me and took another swig. He sat the jug

down and picked up the bucket. "You know, boy, this ol' still was my pappy's before me and has seen it's best days."

He looked like he was gettin' a pretty good buzz on and was in better humor than I'd seen him in to date. I said, "Can't you get some new plumbin' to fix the leaks?"

"I done that before I fired it up. I borrowed -you might say," he grinned like the village idiot, "some money from another 'shiner that I figured he didn't need no more." He waved at the big copper tank. "The plumbin' ain't the problem now, it's that tank. It's plumb worn out."

"Can you buy another one?"

He glared at me. "Stop your jawin', boy. and get to choppin'." By mid-afternoon, he'd guzzled well over a jug and a half but didn't seem to be gettin' much drunker. I never seen nothin' like it. 'Bout dusk, I saw Epidus at the edge of the trees lookin' as forlorn as a toothless Coyote. I glanced over to Luke and saw him walkin' toward the river. I frantically waved Ep' back into the woods. She dropped her tail 'tween her legs and backed off.

Luke returned from the river with a fish on a line and dropped it in his bucket. He waved at us. "It's gettin' too dark. Take this here fish and hustle us up some supper."

Once in the cabin, I whispered to Katie, "Did'ja see Ep'?"

"No. Where was she?"

"She's hangin' out watchin' us from the woods."

"Oh, the poor thing."

"Ep'l be alright. She gets by right fine by herself in the woods." I spotted a box of grits on an upper shelf. "I'll stoke the stove, Katie. You get us some water in a pan. We're gonna have grits with our fish tonight."

Once I had the fire goin', I checked to be sure Luke was still outside and whispered into Katie's ear. "On the good side, I didn't see Luke lookin' funny at you none at all today."

Katie smiled. "His only interest seems to be making and drinking moonshine."

I grinned, "He only manages to make a little more than he drinks. He's not much of a business man."

I was droppin' the filleted fish into the bubblin' fat when Luke slammed into the cabin. His face was flushed and sweaty. "Gotta admit it. With you two helpin'', we made twice the 'shine today than I could of by myself."

"Glad we could be of assistance," I said like a butt kisser.

Luke put on his 'village idiot' grin and lurched back out the door toward the doorless outhouse. Katie kept her eyes glued on the grits she was stirrin'. When Luke returned, I decided it was time for me to get him talkin'. I looked over my shoulder and said, "Luke, it was mighty uncomfortable tryin' to sleep in that smokehouse. Would you let us sleep outside tonight? We wouldn't run off or nothin'. We couldn't. I swear we was right lost when you found us."

Luke flopped into a chair and glared at me. "Don't press your luck with me, boy." Then he laughed. "Hell, if it weren't for me, you'all would be alligator crap by now. I'm keepin' you in the smokehouse for your own protection."

I tried to keep a friendly conversation goin' durin' dinner without much success. He wanted to just eat and drink. As soon as we'd rinsed the dishes he locked us back in the smokehouse for the night.

The night before, I'd felt all over the floor in the dark for anything I could use to try to slip in the crack of the door to drop the latch, but the room was plumb empty. Once I heard Luke walk away, I got flatout depressed. It didn't look like I was gonna have no success gettin' Luke to drink himself to sleep tonight or any night.

We could hear him fussin' around outside for 'bout an hour and then his door slammed and the night went deathly quiet. I was just dozin' off with my back to the door, when I heard a whine outside.

"It's Ep'," I whispered to Katie and suddenly had an escape plan dumped into my lap. I jumped to my feet and stood

135

against the door and whispered to Ep', "Up, girl." I'd taught her to stand on her hind legs to beg for treats ever since she was a pup. Ep' whined again and I could hear her bouncin' around on her hind legs and scratchin' the door with her front paw claws.

"Over here, Ep'," I said and tapped where I knew the latch was.

Ep' didn't understand and dropped back onto all fours. I was as nervous as a long-tailed cat in a room of rockin' chairs that Luke was gonna hear the commotion and come out. It didn't matter. This was our only chance and I had to push on with Ep'. I tapped the door again and said, "Up, Ep', up."

I heard her stand and scratch the door again.

"Over here, Ep', over here." My voice was drippin' desperation. Ep' danced along the outside of the door, unsure of what I wanted her to do. I kept tappin' where the door latch was and started pushin' on the door. She dropped back onto all fours and whined.

"Up, Ep', up," I pleaded and scratched my fingernails against the door while I pushed. She whined again, stood and started frantically clawing against the door. It sounded loud enough to wake the whole dang swamp and I was plumb scared but determined.

All of a sudden, one of her paws hit the latch, down it went and I slammed the door open. Fresh air and Ep' poured into the room. I hugged her briefly and whispered to Katie, "Grab up Buffy and lets get to the boat!"

The four of us took off across the yard like rats up a rafter. I stopped momentarily and peeked into Luke's bedroom window. He was still dressed and passed out crossways on his bed. He wasn't gonna notice us leavin'. He wouldn'ta noticed the Creature from the Black Lagoon leavin'.

In an owl's blink, Katie and the dogs was in my boat and I was pushin' it off from shore.

Katie whispered, "Ep', you were terrific." She smiled at me as I jumped into the boat. "You were too, Robby."

I poled us out into the current. Katie said, "Which way are you going, Robby? We were lost when Luke found us."

I pulled the well-worn sack outta my pocket. "Here's where Smokey said his brother lived."

I placed a finger on a point on the map. "That's where we are!"

Katie made a dive for our belongin's stuffed in the tarp and outta sight under the bow. Katie grabbed up the compass and pointed. "Then pole us right up that channel."

I poled away and within a few yards, the jungle ingulfed us. The hammock breathed life through the moss-hung forest and swamp and cypress. We could make out a golden glow through a magnolia tree's broad leaves shinin' like dark polished jade. For the first hour after that, the river ran swiftly under overhangin' butterwoods and swamp laurel. It eddied against the bank that was riotous with white spider lillies. Suddenly thunder boomed above a gray curtain movin' across the piney woods. Small things scurried across dry pine needles on the bank. A water moccasin seekin' the safety of the water, slid down the bank like oil and swam away. A gale hit us movin' its scale until its voice was a high pitched whine. I saw a gray sheet of rain comin' our way and poled to shore.

At dusk, the downpour stopped as abruptly as it had started and was replaced for a time with light drizzle that caused us to shiver. We pulled the tarp around our shoulders. The drizzle stopped after a bit and the night turned musical as a multitude of frogs piped up and down their organs. Swarms of mosquitoes settled on us like a cloud. I buttoned up my shirt, squinted down my eyes and pressed my lips tight together to keep the bugs outta my neck, eyes and mouth. Bats darted to and from their roosts with whistling wings.

A full moon finally came up as white as the belly of a dead fish and the four of us crashed under the tarp.

137

CHAPTER 21

The sun was full up when I spotted the switchin' yard through a grove of pines. I pulled the boat partly onto the shore and tied it to a tree.

"Come on, Katie. Let's find Smokey!"

The four of us walked through the trees and across the yard to Smokey's caboose.

"Smokey! Are you in there?" I yelled.

No answer.

I knocked on the door. "Are you there?"

Still no answer.

I opened the door a crack and peeked in. The caboose was empty.

"I guess he's on another toot." I slowly exhaled.

Katie's nose wrinkled at the stale bachelor smell of the caboose. "What are we going to do?"

I said, "We'll stay here and wait for him."

"Oh, Robby. This is going to be so much fun!" Katie

hugged me. I slammed open all the empty cabinets and said, "I'm hungrier than a woodpecker with a headache.
I've got seventeen bucks. What'cha got in the cigar box?"

"Close to a hundred."

I raised my eyebrows. "I don't feel right waitin' for Smokey in his caboose. Come on, I gotta idea."
Katie followed me over to the freight car I'd arrived in four days before and I slid the door open.

"We'll make our home in here 'til Smokey gets back."
Katie looked dubiously into the dim interior.

I said, "I'll go into Smithtown and get some supplies. You stay here in case Smokey shows up."

An hour later, I'd purchased a pull wagon at the hardware store and loaded it with a Coleman campin' stove, lantern, ice chest, block of ice, food and other supplies. I pulled it back down the tracks to the yard and deposited it all into the freight car. Katie did a survey of my purchases and nodded approvingly. I looked around the yard and saw an abandoned rusty track headin' into heavy foliage.

"I'm gonna hide the car down that track." I pointed. "I don't want us out in the open if Luke or somebody else shows up." "How are you going to move it, Robby?" Katie put her hands on her hips.

"Just watch me," I smiled and headed toward the shed. I returned with the engine's key and control handles. I pushed them into the cab and swung myself up the steps.

"Come on in, Katie."

"You're going to drive this train?" Katie blinked.

I squatted in front of the battery compartment and flipped on the main battery switch. A minute later, I climbed into the engineer's seat and inserted the key.

"Whew, is there anything you can't do, Robby?" Katie asked as I slid the control handles into place. Her comment made me feel real manly and I'm afraid I probably beamed a little.

I reached up and turned on the fuel pump and waited for

139

the pressure to build up.

"Cross your fingers, Katie." I pushed the starter button. The diesel promptly started. The run into Clancy and back had totally recharged the batteries. Katie was wide-eyed as she watched the brake's air pressure gauges rise.

"Let's hook up to our new home, Katie." I yelled above the engine noise and shoved the reverser handle to the left.

A few minutes later, I backed the engine into the freight car and made connection. I jumped down from the cab, closed a valve, and hooked up the train brake air hose from the engine to the car like Smokey'd told me.

"I'll be right back," I said. "I'm gonna leave Smokey a note."

A couple of minutes later, I climbed back into the cab and slowly pushed the throttle forward. I yelled, "Let's go home!"

Katie, stood behind me and threw her arms around my neck.

"Okay!"

The freight car pushed into the thick foliage that closed back over the tracks after the engine had backed into it. I kept the throttle down to an eight mile per hour speed while leanin' out the window to watch the track ahead. The banks was dense with honeysuckle.

Three miles down the track, we crossed an old wooden bridge over a large channel of clear water. The channel fed into a river that emptied into the gulf.

A mile later, I saw a barrier ahead indicatin' that the tracks was unusable beyond. I pulled the throttle back and pumped the engine brake handle the way I'd seen Smokey do it.

"Let's go back and park the car by the bridge where the track's all overgrown," I said. "We'll be totally hidden from the switchin' yard and next to clean water."

An hour later, we returned the switchin' engine to the yard and kicked dirt onto the metal now scratched and shinin' through the rusty track that led out through the thick foliage to our hideout. Back at the bridge, we scrubbed out the interior of the car and set up housekeepin'. At dusk, when the fish was bitin', we sat 'neath the bridge and within ten minutes I had a fish on the line. Katie clapped her hands together as I gently encouraged the fish toward shore.

"Don't let him get loose," Katie said.

"I been fishin' since I shed my folded three-cornered pants," I said. We cleaned and filleted the fish and made hushpuppies.
Her face was pink in the light of the Coleman stove. After we turned the gas off the stove, it got so dark the bats stayed home.

The followin' day, we moved our boat through meanderin' waterways to the bridge and hid it under an overlyin' and impeneratable blackberry bush in the deep shadows under the bridge, we walked down to the switchin' yard to see if Smokey had returned. No luck.

We saw the first cloud cross over the sun and scurried home. We knew the cloud would soon spread until the sky was gray and the air would become hot, humid and still. Suddenly an impalpable breath stirred the moss in the hammock followed by rain marchin' visibly toward us in a rushin' flood. We ran leanin' against the force of the rain to the shelter of our freight car. We listened to the hooves of rain beat on the roof.

Afterwards, the air cooled and we came out to look at the serenity of the river and watch its colors change from vivid greens and blues to a modest bed of subdued gold as the sun set across it. We took my shotgun out lookin' for dinner. I saw a small wild turkey rufflin' through the tall grass and shot it. Katie took it back to boil it and pluck its feathers. I scoured the adjacent hammock for wild mustard greens, collard greens and edible swamp cabbage. We made an outstandin' turkey stew for dinner with a mango and two wild plums for desert.

After dinner, we decided to walk down to the river and take a swim in our undies to clean up. On the way, I spotted a low -growin' plant in the moonlight. It had tube-like leaves that Eloise had taught me 'bout. "I want you to see this, Katie." I said and split a leaf open. The inner leaf revealed piles of dead gnats, mites, chiggars, spiders and beetles. Katie's eyes opened wide. "Yuck. What is that thing?"

I laughed, "It's called a carnivorous plant. It traps and feeds off of insects."

Katie shuddered. "I'm not sure we're in a very safe place."

It was cool that night and the hoards of mosquitos stayed mostly in the swamp, so we stayed down by the river. I said,

"Eloise told me years ago a pirate named Henry Morgan used to pull his ship into the Aucilla river whenever he was on the run."

I put my arm around Katie. "The Seminoles believe you can still see his phantom ship sailin' through on full moon nights."

"I love this place, Robby. But it's pretty scary."

CHAPTER 22
Dr. Newton's Story Continued:

I sure can't fault the good people of Newton. They scoured every foot of ground in every direction from sunup to sundown. They didn't find a trace of my girl although they came across one couple in a pretty compromising position, so far out in the boondocks they probably never dreamed anybody'd come along and catch them in such an embarrasing state.

It took me two days to set up getting onto television with an appeal. But, on the fifth day since my girl turned up missing, I drove up to Tallahassee and made an appeal on Florida television for her to come home. I also offered a $10,000 reward for any news about her whereabouts. When I got back home to Newton, it was pretty late and I was pretty tired. Climbing out of my Buick, Ed McKinley stepped out of the shadows.

"Evenin', Doctor."

"What are you doing here, Ed?" I stepped out of my car.

"I got a call three days ago from Major Swagert up at

Fort Pulaski. He's the head soldier boy there."

"I know," I said and waited anxiously for what Ed had to say.

"Well, he done told me my boy was a'missin'. Had been for several days."

I did some day-counting arithmetic in my head and realized the Major had told me a boldface lie when I'd called him.

"Told me my boy had been kidnapped by some Cuban crooks from Miami."

"Baloney!" I slammed the car door.

"It was baloney alright." Ed jingled some change in his pocket. "On my way out, one of the senior kind of cadets was waitin' for me outside the school. He told me that the soldier boy had made it so tough on my boy tryin' to run him outta the school ... well, my boy had to pull up stakes and -" I interrupted.

"When was that?"

"Goin' on a week, I calculate. Anyhow, this senior cadet helped my boy jump a freight train headin' for Valdosta."

I put my hands on my hips. "Where have you been the last three days?"

"I drove to Valdosta and searched every park and bus station, talked to every fast food joint-well, just name it and I looked there."

"Did you find anything?"

"Not there, but I did in Clancy. My boy had ham and eggs there five days ago."

"Hop in the car," I said. "He's with my Katie by now. Let's see if they're hiding out at your place."

On the way to Ed's house, I told him about Katie being missing and why. He deserved to know the part I'd played and I told him everything up front and honest.

There was no trace of them at Ed's house and he commented, "Ol Ep' still ain't come home either."

"Ep'? Your boy's dog is missing?"

"Oh, she got loose from her rope a couple a days before

I got the call from Savannah. I expected her home by now."

"Oh, God, Ed. Our kids are together right now for sure, along with both their dogs."

"How do you know?" He asked and I told him.

"Where do you think they'd be?" I asked.

"I don't know, but Eloise might."

The lights of my Buick woke up Eloise as I pulled up in front of her cabin. As soon as we were out of the car, she opened the front door with an old robe pulled around her. I took a few minutes and explained the whole situation before asking, "Would you have any idea where they might be?

Eloise answered, "Is Robby's boat missin'?"

"It was slowly sinkin' into the river last I seen it," Ed answered. "Still tied to a stump however."

I gasped, "Do you think he'd take them into the swamp?"

"He was hell bent on checkin' thet swamp out." Eloise shook her head. "If they's missin', and you haven't had no luck findin' no traces on dry ground. I's horribly afraid they's gone into thet swamp!"

CHAPTER 23

Rob's Story Continued:

On the next morning in our new home, I got up before the others and poled the flat-bottom out to the deepest spot in the channel where I'd dropped my catfish line the day before. I wanted to surprise Katie with a catfish for breakfast. I grabbed the line and started to draw it into the boat. It wouldn't move. I realized it was snagged on somethin' and tugged unsuccessfully.

After a few minutes, I sat down on the cross beam and took off my shoes. That line and hook was too precious to lose. I slid over the side and swam quickly to the bottom. I found the hook snagged on a flat-bottom boat. As I started to pull it out, I noticed a hole in the bottom of the boat big enough to put your foot through. It was then, through the muddy water, I seen a huge fat man standin' and grinnin' at me at the other end of the boat. I shot to the surface and must'a looked like a seal slam bangin' back into my boat. I frantically poled away for a couple of minutes and looked back. Nobody had surfaced. I knew then the man in the boat was bloated dead and that was why he was floatin' like he was.

I slowly poled back to the site. I sure needed the hook and line, but I also didn't relish goin' back down to get it. "Well, he's dead," I said to myself.

I dove over the side.

As I worked the hook loose outta the side of the boat, I looked at the body. It was dressed in Levi trousers and a denim shirt that ruffled slowly in the dark bottom current. A large sand-filled glass jug lyin' on the channel floor was wired to one of its ankles.

"You won't believe what I found down there!" I yelled to Katie as I poled under the bridge. Back on shore and breath-less, I told 'bout the body.

"Was it a skeleton?" Katie asked, her eyes wild with excitement.

"No. He ain't been there that long. He's weighted down with a glass jug. Otherwise he'd of floated to the surface he was so bloated standin' there like a balloon. He looked like he was grinnin' at me."

Katie shuddered. "Then it sounds like he was murdered recently."

"He's been there more than a few days," I said.

Katie said. "I bet it's that moonshiner Luke said had disappeared."

I nodded agreement. "The guy he 'borrowed' money from. This has Luke's handwritten' all over it alright."

Katie put an arm around my waist. "I think this place is a lot more dangerous than just having carnivorous plants. Your friend just has to get here right away."

We took a fruitless run down to the switchin' yard and, later made chowder from crabs boiled in salt water. After we ate, the air was cool and we looked down at the serenity of the river and watched its colors change from vivid greens and blues to a modest bed of subdued gold as the sun humbly set across it. Twilight overflowed the river and flooded across the train tracks.

We climbed the metal ladder to the roof of the car and talked excitedly about the body I'd discovered.

I was awakened from the dark caverns of sleep that night by Buffy's high-pitched yappin' at the door. I raised up and nudged Katie.

"What is it!" She leaped up.

"Do you hear that?" I asked.

Katie put her ear close to the door. "It sounds like an airplane."

We stood and looked out from the top of the car. A smell of pine resin mixed with a faint smell of the sea drifted by. At first we didn't see nothin' 'cept moonlight fallin' in ivory squares across the channel. Then, Katie nudged me and pointed toward a single cloud hangin' low in the sky. I saw a flashlight beam movin' back and forth across it.

Suddenly, a two-engine plane with pontoons glided toward us into the channel. It settled in a whoosh in the dark green water and came to a stop. Small waves lapped at the pontoons.

"Ep, Buff," I called down. "be quiet." I turned to Katie. "That plane is sittin' just 'bout where I dived and found the body."

A boat was poled slowly out of the blackened mist at the edge of the channel.

"It must be those moonshiners Mr. Crafton talked about," Katie whispered.

"Yeah, and that's Rusty Yates comin' in the plane to make a moonshine pick-up. Let's get closer and see what's goin' on."

I put the dogs in the car and takin' Katie's hand, ventured into the inky night. The light of the moon first illuminated a green tree toad lookin' unblinkingly at us. A few yards further on, a black snake, a slimy ebony beauty with a smooth raven head held high above the dark grass, watched us. We skirted around it. We got as close as we dared and squatted in the rush grass. As the boat poled up to the plane, Rusty called out, "Howdy, Larry." Larry Zitterkoph looking like he fell outta the

148

ugly tree and hit every branch on the way down, maneuvered his boat up parallel to one of the pontoons and tied both ends up tight.

"You seen Bill Dooley or Luke?" Rusty asked.

"No, I shore haven't," Larry answered.

"I'm here," a voice called out not twenty yards from where we was hid. I, for one, just about shed my skin like a molted snake. Katie's finger nails slammed into my arm like five little staples.

"That you Luke?" Rusty called out.

Luke poled his boat over to the other pontoon and tied up in a similar manner. "You got the money?"

"Of course," Rusty said. He looked real nervous. "Let's load up, Larry."

For the next few minutes, Larry would load a full five gallon jug into a Bonita banana box and then slide the box into the body of the plane. Rusty would replace the full bottle with an empty he's brought with him. When they was finished, Rusty said, "I counted twelve jugs, you agree?"

Larry nodded.

Rusty then climbed out onto the other pontoon. He did a double take, and then said, "This all you got, Luke? Just five jugs?"

Luke answered, "I had me some troubles. You got a problem with it?"

Rusty looked like he was squirmin'. "No, of course not, Luke. I'm just the pick-up and delivery man."

"Then start pickin' up," Luke said.

As Rusty put the first empty replacement into Lukes's boat, he cleared his throat and said, "I've got a message for you from Crafton."

"Yeah, what is it? Luke grunted.

"The doctor's girl and a boy found out about our operation."

Luke let a jug slip back to the bottom of his boat. "That

149

idiot Crafton!"

"The doctor ordered Crafton to shut down the operation." Rusty said.

"Then, why is you here?" Luke stopped unloadin' and put his hands on his hips. Rusty said, "'Cause the doctor never was the real boss, he just thought he was. This bottlin' and distributin' moonshine was Crafton's idea from the get go. He talked the doctor into it to save the soft drink bottlin' business. Crafton knew several distributors around sellin' a little 'shine on the side. He knew he could set them up to start distributin' a lot of 'shine. Crafton played the doctor for a sucker. Here, let me give you a hand with that."

Rusty helped Luke wrestle a boxed jug out of the boat. Rusty continued: "We shut down all right. But what the doctor don't know is we moved all the equipment to my place and started up again. Crafton told me to tell you, Dooley and Larry our whole plan because you, and the rest of the swamp 'shiners are critical to our success."

Rusty handed down Luke an empty jug and said, "Crafton figures on runnin' the legit bottlin' into the ground. He's been skimmin' off the top ever since Newton got the Dr. Pepper franchise. If he hadn't," Rusty laughed, "the plant wouldn't of had no financial problem. Crafton's gonna tell Newton he's inherited some money and wants to buy the franchise off him.

"The doctor's so sick of the whole mess, he'll sell for a song. He's frantic now 'cause his girl turned up missin' the night she saw the operation in the barn. With a bill of sale signed by the doctor, Crafton will have him right where he wants him. The doctor will have to keep his mouth shut."

Rusty grunted and shoved the box into the plane.

"Anyhow, all the doctor can think about now is finding his daughter."

Luke said, "Well, he ain't gonna find her. She and that boy is lost in this swamp."

"You seen 'em?" Rusty asked.

"I seen 'em." Luke answered.

Rusty said, "Crafton says they're the only threat we got toward havin' a successful operation."

Luke grunted, "I 'spect they're alligator crap by now."

A few minutes later, the transfer was complete except for one jug in the far end of Luke's boat. A little coil of bailin' wire was beside it.

Luke said, "That's it, let's see the color of your money."

Rusty lit a cigarette and nodded at the remainin' jug."

"How about that one?"

"Not for sale. It's filled full of sand as ballast for my boat." Luke leered. "Let's have the money."

Rusty counted out a number of bills and handed them to Luke. He turned and did the same to Larry.

"I wonder what the hell happened to Dooley?" he said.

Larry answered, "I ain't seen him since Luke helped him make the last delivery. You'all seen him, Luke?"

Luke grunted, "No, been too busy makin' 'shine."

Rusty flicked his cigarette into the water and without another word, ducked back into the plane. In a minute, the plane's propellers rotated and the plane taxied into a turn. Rusty slammed the throttle forward and the propellers raised a wake of waves behind it as it took to the air. The commotion caused a bunch of bats to sweep off the limbs above us and dart and dive around with their wings whistlin'.

Luke said, "Hey, Larry, ol' buddy. I brought along a flask to keep me company on the pole home. Care for a snort?" Before Larry could move his boat, Luke reached across his bow and rope tied the two boats together. Larry didn't look pleased.

"You'all not willin' to share a bottle with me?" Luke sounded threatenin'.

Larry hesitated a little longer and then seemed to decide he didn't have no choice and said, "Shore, Luke. Toss it over to me."

Luke stepped up onto his bow and jumped gracefully into

Larry's boat and caught his balance as the boat rocked. "It's no good for us to be throwin' the bottle back and forth. I'll just join you." He held the boat's side with one hand and poured moonshine down his throat from the bottle in his other hand. When he was through, he wiped the back of his hand across his mouth and handed the bottle to Larry. "Here's to us bein' business partners, Larry, ol' buddy."

Larry reached out for the bottle with one hand. His other was holdin' somethin' in his pocket. He was very careful not to get too close to Luke. The instant Larry tilted his head back to drink, Luke stepped gracefully forward, his hand flashed out of his pocket and a switchblade flashed open. Larry threw the bottle at Luke's head and tried to yank something outta his own pocket. Luke shoved his switchblade deep into Larry's chest. Larry dropped an unopened jackknife he'd pulled outta his pocket and grabbed with both hands at Luke's knife's handle and seemed to be tryin' to pull it out. Luke stepped back and said, "Sorry ol' buddy, but you see, I need your still."

Larry slumped down to the bottom of the boat where we couldn't see him no more. But we could hear his death rattle; he sounded as dead as a can of corn beef.

It only took Luke a minute to grab Larry's money, lean into his boat for the sandfilled jug and wire the jug to Larry's ankle. Luke then poled Larry's boat, with his boat draggin', to the deepest part of the channel. He pulled up and began stompin' on the boat's floor until he made a hole. He waited watchin' water pourin' into the boat and then untied the rope connectin' the two boats and stepped back into his own boat.

After Luke turned his boat toward home, I shakily whispered to Katie, "That's the same place I found the body."

Katie said, "The body has to be Mr. Dooley's."

I said, "If Smokey doesn't show up tomorrow, I'm takin' you home." I hugged her to me. "We're too close to Luke's shippin', receivin' and private cemetary."

Katie said, "Daddy isn't in the moonshine business anymore and he's real worried about me."

I suddenly realized what she was saying. "We can go on home and tell your pa what Crafton's plan is."

Katie said, "I'm scared to death to go back into the swamp. Luke will catch us for sure."

I thought for a minute. "We don't have to. We can go into Smithtown and call your pa to come pick us up."

Katie nodded real excited like and said, "His office is closed now, and I don't want to risk getting my mom on our home line if daddy isn't there. She doesn't know anything about this business."

"She might just call Crafton to come help her," I said.

Katie agreed. "We have to wait until after nine in the morning and call daddy's office. Nobody else can find out where we are except daddy. He's the only one we can trust."

CHAPTER 24

Real early the next mornin', I gathered up my fishin' pole and the shotgun, looked around a bit for ghosts, and then moseyed nervously down to the channel bank. After what we'd seen last night, I wasn't lettin' the shotgun outta my sight. I dropped the fishin' line in to catch our breakfast. Katie rolled up our sleepin' bags and started lightin' the Coleman camp stove to heat water.

Epidus, always happy in the early mornin', went on her search of daily treasures. She almost always returned by midday with shiny eyes bearin' some strange trophy like a lizard or small snake.

Buffy had hated the backwoods from the first sandspur under her tail and spent her days hangin' out at the door of the car and only ventured as far as the water when she was thirsty. This mornin', she sniffed the air and decided to get a drink. About half way to the water, she sniffed, looked into the brush and began to bark her fool head off. I doggone near dropped my pole.

I looked into the brush and saw the problem; a thirsty

bobcat stopped in its tracks by Buffy's barkin'. The bobcat braced its front legs and hissed in preparation to spring on Buffy if Buffy got any closer. Well, Buffy like every little dog you ever saw, didn't have enough sense to know she wasn't tough enough to take on this cat which was as big as Ep'.

I didn't want to hurt the cat none, but I sure didn't want him jumpin' Buffy, so I dropped the pole and fired the shotgun into the ground. That cat done sprang sideways and took off like its tail was on fire.

Katie came outta the car and yelled, "What is it?"

"Just a bobcat Buffy was about to tear limb from limb," I said. Katie called the dog and grabbed her up just as Ep' arrived back in camp to find out what all the noise was about.

Katie said, "Let's skip breakfast, Robby and just get on to Smithtown."

I nodded agreement and pointed to the dogs. "Let's leave these guys in the car until we get back. I don't want nothin' else to happen to them."

I pointed to the car and ordered Epidus in. She cocked one ear and looked up into my eyes. She didn't understand why she was being locked in the car.

Katie and I took off down the track. When we got to the switchin' yard I called out, "Smokey?" My answer was a lone mockingbird makin' his song in a chinaberry tree nearby. I looked around but saw no signs that Smokey had returned. We headed on down the tracks to Smithtown. A wind kicked up and spat sand in our faces. There was a smell of pine resin in the wind.

I'd been thinkin' as we trudged along. "Katie, we're still not outta the woods. If Crafton finds out where we are before your pa gets here, him and Rusty's liable to show up. I don't think you ought'a be the one callin' the doctor's office 'cause the receptionist will recognize your voice and if your daddy isn't there, she'll put the word out you're in Smithtown. I'd better make the call."

"That's a good idea. And Katie thought for a moment. "Don't you suppose the people of Smithtown know we're missing?"

I saw where she was goin' and said, "If they see the two of us they'll know who we are and call people in Newton. You better go back and wait in the trainyard and I'll go in by myself."

I was back in forty minutes. Katie jumped up from sittin' on the track. "Did you talk to daddy?"

"No, his receptionist told me he's out following down leads lookin' for you. He won't be back to his office until four o'clock this afternoon."

Katie sighed, "Then we may as well go back and wait with the dogs."

I said, "Let's stop and leave a new note for Smokey just in case he shows up today."

Half an hour later, we rounded the last bend in the tracks and heard the dogs barkin' in the distance.

"It sounds like Buffy and Epidus are pretty unhappy with us leaving them behind," Katie commented.

I took her hand as we walked along. She looked up at me. "I'm already missing you."

I stopped dead on the tracks, turned and kissed her. We hugged lost in our innermost thoughts. Even now as I tell it, light years since that moment, I warmly shudder thinkin' about it.

A crack of thunder jolted us back to earth, and we walked the last hundred yards to our car. I noticed that the flatwoods that had been sunny and populous with birds had grown dense and dark. "Looks like we've got another storm comin' up."

I climbed down the bank and pushed into the tall grass to get the shotgun. Suddenly the breeze stopped and there was no breath of coolness anywhere. The yellow-grayness of the sky was tinted with green. I heard the now familiar low roar of the comin' wind, like a train thunderin' nearer and nearer. The palmettos started thrashin' their fans in a frenzy.

It always surprised me how quickly these storms came up. I shoved aside a cypress branch and prepared to slide down the muddy bank to retrieve our boat hidden under the overhang. The mixed stink of alcohol and a dirty body hit me just before a hand, smelling of tobacco, slammed over my mouth.

CHAPTER 25
Smokey Tells His Story:

"Shake a leg, Smokey." My engineer friend, Ralph Welter nudged my ribs with a toe of his boot.

"Where ... am I?" I rolled over on the floor of the freight car. It was so quiet you could hear the daylight coming.

"I found you again last night passed out at a table in that dive in Charleston. You were so hammered you couldn't hit your hat on the ground in three tries." Ralph helped me to my feet. "I brought you home this morning."

I grabbed both sides of my head and moaned.

Ralph said, "Smokey, I've been ordered to take all the old cars to the repair depot up in Valdosta."

Ralph was still in his twenties and jumped easily to the ground. When I hesitated, he reached back and gave me a hand down. "I've already picked up everything except your caboose."

"Ah hell. There goes my happy home."

"I can wait a spell on the caboose."

"Don't pee down my back and tell me it's a rainin'."

"I'm laying over in Smithtown 'til this evening."

Ralph grabbed a railing and swung himself up onto the engine's walkway. "Loading up a couple of cars with pecans to take on to Valdosta tonight. You can ride with me, if you want." He was as honest as a looking glass but not one to get stuck on the blister end of a shovel. "I doubt you'll be doin' the loading yourself."

"Course not. I'll get a loader. You can find me in the Smithtown Cafe till sundown."

"I'll think on it. See ya' later."

The short train backed out of the yard and I walked across the track to the caboose. I opened the door and sat down on the cot by a folded sack. I unfolded it and read:

Hi Smokey,

It's Rob. I've got my friend Katie with me. We're staying in a car down the rusty tracks across the way. We need your help pretty bad. It's about noon on Friday and we're pulling out this evening. If you get back this afternoon, I'd sure be obliged if you'd drop by. Your friend,

Rob

"Now, ain't that something." I dropped the sack onto the cot.

"The little rascal pulled off stealing his girlfriend from her pappy."

Forty-five minutes later, I rounded the last bend before the bridge. I could see Rob's freight car parked in the shadows on the far side of the bridge and could hear the muffled yapping of a little dog mixed with the deep barking of a bigger one. It was coming from the car's interior. Movement caught my eye down the slope close to the water.

A big man dressed in overalls was in the process of tyin' somebody up on the ground. The man looked alot like Luke, although it'd been a few years since I'd see'd him. I climbed down the track bank and moved with what I thought was Seminole quiet and grace along the shrubbery. My headache was suddenly repaired by an injection of adrenaline.

In a hundred yards, I slid behind the car and peeked around

a corner and caught my breath. Luke had Robby's hands tied behind his back and was draggin' him and a beautiful girl in her early teens toward an old flat-bottom boat tied to a stump on the shore. The girl was dressed in pants and a tattered blouse. Her hair fanned out around her head like a golden pillow. I see'd that Luke had a gun stuffed into his pants. The frantic dog barkin' drowned all sounds and thunder roared behind my eyes.

"You sonuvabitch," I whispered and raced down the slope and threw myself onto Luke. We tumbled into the water. I got a headlock on his neck with my right arm and smashed short blows into his ugly face with my left. Luke's eyes were wild and he pulled at my choking arm with both hands. We slid under the surface and wrestled around for the better part of a minute.

Luke surfaced first and took a giant gulp of air just as I raised up and sank a fist deep into his belly. "Oh!" Luke gasped.

I took a deep breath and slammed a fist into the side of his jaw. A rotten tooth flew out and splashed into the water. Luke was slipping and sliding and tryin' to get a hand on his gun. He pulled it out of his pants but I got hold of the barrel and twisted it outta his hand. I always was the stronger. I pulled it back and felt a knife go deep into my side. I gasped as Luke pulled it out.

"I think I finally done killed you big brother," Luke smiled that crazy smile of his through bloody teeth. "Jes to be sure, I'm a going to cut ya' some more."

He stepped forward and I slammed the gun butt up side his head. Luke's eyes rolled back and he collapsed in the water. I caught my breath for a time. "Ya'll okay, Rob?" I grunted.

"I shore am now that you're here." Robby was grinnin' from ear to ear. The girl was busy untyin' his ropes.

"Ya'll must be Katie," I said.

"And you must be Smokey. I saw Luke stick his knife into you!"

Rob was slippin' outta the ropes. I said, "Rob, give me a hand pullin' this hyena to shore. We gotta get him hogtied before he comes around."

While Rob was transferrin' his ropes to Luke, I inspected the damage Luke had done me; a crimson lake was spreading across my khaki shirt. Katie slid open the door and two dogs leaped out ready to tear out my windpipe. Katie yelled, "No, this is Robby's friend, Smokey!" The big dog ran to Rob and the little dog looked doubtful but obeyed.

Rob finished up tyin' Luke and turned to me with a horrified look on his face. "Oh God, Smokey! You're hurt bad."

I said, "I am feelin' a mite dizzy."

Katie tore open my shirt and looked at the wound.

"We've got to get you to a doctor as fast as we can, Smokey." She turned to Rob. "I'll get the towels out of the boat. I've got to wrap this wound as tight as I can." She looked back at me. "The only way out for you is to walk. Are you up to it?"

"I guess I have to be."

While Katie was wrapping my wound, I winked at Rob. "You've got a real take charge kind'a girlfriend here." I noticed a flicker of a smile on Katie's face before she caught herself.

An hour later, I staggered into the yard leaned on both Katie and Rob. I collapsed onto the cot in the caboose. "I cain't go no further."

"Robby, we've got to get him to a doctor within an hour or he's going to bleed to death." Katie was pushing hard on the blood soaked towels. "I can't stop the bleeding ... daddy's the closest doctor this side of Tallahassee."

Rob told me later, he'd run to the switching engine and jumped aboard. The key was still in place where he'd left it. He hit the starter and the engine slowly turned over and stopped. He hit the starter again. It turned over even slower and then stopped and just clicked. I guess he must'a left some switch on after he last used the engine. The batteries was dead.

Robby jumped down and yelled over to Katie, "You stay with Smokey. I'll run into Smithtown for help." Rob darted to the door and turned.

"Ep', Buff', stay and guard Katie and Smokey."

CHAPTER 26

Rob's Story Continued:

Dark clouds spread across the afternoon sky and rain started to pelt my face as I ran into Smithtown. The single main street was empty and the first buildin' I come to was the hardware store. I slammed through the door.

"I need help." I caught my breath and gasped.

"What' cha need, boy." An elderly, hunched and skinny store keeper looked skeptically me.

"A friend of mine needs a doctor. He's been knifed."

"Where is he?"

"A mile or so down the track in the old switchin' yard."

The old man shook his head. "There ain't no sawbones in Smithtown. We'all go to Tallahassee if'n we need one."

"I need transportation for him now," My voice was shakin'. "Or he's going to die."

"I ain't got no vehicle. Tom Day has an old pickup over at the general store." The old man pointed out the window.

I ran back out into the rain and crossed the street.

"Lordy boy. Ya'll look like you're 'bout to have a stroke," A fat mulatto in his late forties exclaimed.

"My friend's been knifed and has to get to a doctor right away. The man in the hardware store said you've got a pickup and might help."

"I'm the only one here." The fat man threw up both hands. "My wife's down with a misery. I can't leave the store unattended."

"But my friend's gonna die if he don't get to a doctor in less than an hour."

"If we left right now, we couldn't make it to Tallahassee in under two."

I was shiftin' from one foot to the other. "How about Newton?"

"About the same. There's no direct road to Newton. Got to go north thirty miles to the paved road and then another hour and a half on a bunch of switchbacks from there." The mulatto shook his head. "Sorry, boy, but I don't think I can help you."

I ran back into the downpour and looked frantically up and down the street. All I could see was several pickups randomly parked in front of the town's saloon and an idlin' diesel locomotive billowin' out a mist of vapor in the gray distance.

"A train could get Smokey to Dr. Newton in time." I mouthed. I ran the two blocks to the train bright and clean as a new mirror. I yelled up into the cab. "Hello, anybody there?"

There wasn't nobody.

I ran down the length of the train and found an old Negro stackin' gunny sacks of pecans in one of six freight cars.

"Sir," I yelled into the car. "Do you'all know where I can find the engineer?"

"Don't know where he is." The Negro dropped a sack. "Told me to finish this and he'd be pulling this 'tin lizard' out at six." He picked up the next sack.

I ran to the rear of the train and looked in all directions. The rain was being driven almost horizontally by a wind that had kicked up and leaves and debris swirled around the cars. I wiped my face with the back of my shirt sleeve.

"I don't have the time to look no more," I whispered to myself, and turned and raced to the front of the train.

A magnificent diesel electric locomotive loomed above me, It rumbled like a livin' monster with a cloud of vapor pourin' out its nostrils onto the track from an exhaust manifold. I paused and stared open mouthed; it was at least fifty feet in length and dwarfed the little switchin' engine Smokey had taught me to drive.

I climbed into the closest door and looked squarely at the giant 1,500 horsepower rattlin' idlin' engine. I slammed the door and ran to the left past the main generator and up three metal stairs to an inner door into the cab.

Inside the cab, I looked around the pale green interior. I started to panic; the cab didn't look the same. I took a deep breath and focused on everythin'.

"There's the engineer seat," I sighed and climbed into it. "So, these must be the air brakes." I fondled a platform to my right. "And here's the generator switch." I moved my hand to the engine instrument panel." I breathed deeply and then exhaled. "It's got all the same stuff, just bigger and laid out a little different."

I looked at the floor.

"And there's the deadman's switch." I remembered Smokey mentioned the engineer had to keep it depressed with his foot when the train was movin' or the brakes would lock up and stop the train. It was a safety switch to stop the train if an engineer had a heart attack while drivin'.

Sweat beaded my upper lip.

"The controls aren't in place." I jumped out of the seat and dove for the upper left-hand corner of the cab where Smokey had found the controls in the switchin' engine. There was no box. My heart leaped in my chest and I frantically looked around the cab. There was no place the controls could be stored. Blood pounded in my head like stormy ocean waves against rocks and drowned out the idlin' engine.

"Calm down," I ordered myself. "They've got to be back

in the engine room I just came through."

I jumped down the three stairs and looked around. A metal storage box was to my immediate left. I swung open the door and found the shiny throttle, reverse and brake control handles. I grabbed them up and raced back into the cab and slipped them into place. I looked out the window on my right.

The switchin' yard is behind me, I thought. I've got to back up. I moved the reverse control into the R position, released the handbrake and moved the throttle one indent forward. The train slowly started to move. I remembered that each throttle indent increased the train's speed by four miles per hour.

"Hey you up there!" The Negro from the freight car was runnin' along side. He had a salt and pepper head of steel wool for hair. "What do you think you're doing? Stop the damn train and get down outta there!"

I slid the throttle forward two more indents as the man tried to grab a handle and swing himself up. The train pulled away from him.

"Hot damn! I've done it!" I hollered into the wind.

Within minutes, I saw the switchin' yard through the rain spattered windshield and yanked back the throttle and pumped the air brake handles the way Smokey had showed me. When the train was stopped, I jumped down and ran to the caboose where Katie was standin' outside. She was speechless.

"How's Smokey?" I yelled.

Smokey staggered into the doorway. "I'll dance on your grave." He smiled weakly.

I asked, "Can you walk?" "Sure, if I get a bit of a hand. Ask the engineer to get down here and help me up."

Blood was seepin' down his overalls.

"I'm the engineer, Smokey." I put my shoulder under his armpit. "Lean on me. I've got to get you into the engine compartment."

Smokey's mouth dropped open. "You're the engineer? Boy, did you steal this train?"

I looked up, more than proud. "Just borrowed it long 'nough to get you to Katie's dad." I pushed Smokey toward the engine compartment door. "Let's get to movin'."

Smokey crawled and pulled himself into the engine compartment and flopped onto the floor gaspin' in pain. "Don't forget to switch us onto the Clancy-Newton tracks."

Katie grabbed up Buffy and climbed aboard. Epidus bounded up the steps after her. I leaned out the window on my right and looked ahead. I was worried sick that Smokey would die before I could get him to Dr. Newton. I knew Katie was doing her best to stop the flow of blood comin' outta his belly. But how much blood could he have? The front window was splattered in rain and I didn't know how to engage the wipers. I watched wild red and orange lilies riotin' in the wind flyin' by; hangin' vines looped and tangled into coils off of Hawthorne branches. Shiny pine trees sloughed in the breeze.

Within minutes, the rain suddenly stopped and the wind subsided. The train pulled away from the forest and now pecan farms whizzed by and tall, angular Scotch-Irish 'Cracker' farmers returned to their afternoon toil. I could smell damply sweet grass mixed with the engine exhaust and felt exhilarated. Katie came in through the engine room door.

"Smokey's sleeping. How are you doing?"

"Fine. I should have us into Newton in half an hour."

"Where are the dogs?"

Katie smiled, pointed to the engine room and yelled, "Guarding Smokey". How do you think Luke found us?"

"He musta heard the shotgun when I scared off the bobcat."

Katie said, "This almost seems too easy. Are you sure nobody's chasing us ... like another train? Can't somebody switch the tracks on us up ahead like you did back in the yard?"

I looked into her eyes and nodded my head. "I'll climb up the ladder out on the walkway and see if there's anythin' behind us. Stand on this 'deadman's switch' for a minute. I'll be right back."

I held on to the iron railin's on both sides of the ladder takin' me to the top of the engine. I stood on a rail near the top and turned my head to the rear. I blinked. I thought I'd seen somethin' drop from sight between the second to last and last cars. I stepped up to the next rung but saw nothin' but the swayin' cars behind me and the track was clear as far as I could see. I turned and looked at the track ahead. It was clear too. I took one step down the ladder.

I was carefully lowerin' my right foot down to the next rung as the train swayed around a curve. I held on tight to both rails until the train straightened out and then turned my face out of the wind to the rear. I gasped. Luke's head rose above the surface of the second car.

Luke saw there was no walkways around the freight car, only a metal ladder to the top of the car. He grabbed the ladder rails and carefully climbed to the top. He grasped handholds and looked over the top of the cars ahead. He must'a seen he was on the top of the next to last of six freight cars being pulled by the engine. The car was rockin' and swayin' and the wind must have brought tears to his eyes as it had to mine. He slowly pushed himself erect.

"Watchout, Katie." I pushed her aside and replaced her foot on the deadman's switch with my own. "Luke's on the train." I grabbed the throttle. He's walkin' across the top of the cars coming for us."

"Oh, God, you must not have tied him tight enough!" Katie slammed through the door and climbed the ladder. Luke held both arms out like wings for balance and slid one foot slowly after the other down the center of the car top to the front. He looked at the next car, considered trying to jump to it, and then thought better. He looked between the cars and saw that he could climb down a front ladder of the car he was on, step across the car's couplin', and then climb up a rear ladder on the next car. He swung down the ladder. Katie flew down the steps.

"Robby, you've got to shake him off."

I slammed the throttle all the way forward. The train lurched forward into a curve and Luke fell to his knees and slid forward grabbin' for handholds. He slid over the side feet first and at the last instant grabbed a railin' 'round the edge of the car's top. For several agonizin' seconds, his legs dangled over the side before he could pull himself up, his face in a gargoyle frown.

"Robby, I saw him fall over the side, but he just pulled himself back up. He's not walking anymore though. He's crawling along the top."

"How close is he?"

"He'll be here in two more cars. What can we do?" Katie yelled into the cab.

I pulled back on the throttle and gave the airbrake handle two quick jerks until the train slowed back to a normal speed.

"Here, Katie. Stand on the switch again and keep everything steady until I wave to you. Then goose her."

"What are you going to do?"

"I'm gonna try to disconnect the engine from the rest of the train." I grabbed a pipe wrench wired to the wall.

Katie nodded and stepped onto the switch and took hold of the throttle. Her blond hair swirled about her face.

I walked around the side walkway and lowered myself carefully over the rear. In a minute, I was squattin' over the couplin'. The blurred track seemed only inches below and I had to hold on with one hand as tight as I could to keep from being shaken off.

I saw the couplin's pin and grasped its barlock in my left hand and pulled. It wouldn't budge. I tugged again.

"You little shit."

I looked up into Luke's crazy distorted face. He was on his hands and knees lookin' down on me from the top front of the first freight car connected to the engine. He slid his body over the side and began to climb down.

I swung the pipe wrench with all of my power at the barlock and saw it give a little. Luke's legs was quickly comin' into my vision. I struck again and the pin was pulled. The barlock swung up and I scurried back onto the engine platform. Katie's wild eyes stared at me out the window and her hair streamed along the outside glass. I waved for her to slam the throttle forward.

Luke looked down at the disconnected coupling and saw the engine inchin' away from him as his car started to coast. He leaned back and braced his palms on the cars surface. He looked up at me watchin' him at the engine railin' above. It looked like he was considerin' tryin' to jump to the engine and then chickened out. Luke looked at me with a face contorted into a mask of hate.

I watched him wavin' a fist at me as he got smaller and smaller in the distance.

Moonshine Express

CHAPTER 28
Dr. Newton Continues His Story:

Ed McKinley and I stood on the Newton Train Station platform looking down at half the town's people. The night after we left Eloise, and all damn day yesterday, I called everybody in town with a phone and asked those that had boats to meet us here this afternoon. Ed and I spent a good part of yesterday at the Town Hall looking through the Recording Deed's Map file. We found an old U.S. Geological Survey map of the swamp, spread it out, and spent hours marking out twenty search routes. We then made copies.

We sorted out just who the hell had boats and could help, and who the hell didn't but wanted to help anyway. We asked the boat owners to bunch their boats in the river close to town and then meet us here this afternoon.

I yelled down at the crowd, "Can I have your attention, please. Ed McKinley here is going to hand out maps of the swamp. We've marked them up with twenty different routes, one each for your boats. We have spare horns for those boats without them. If you don't have a horn, don't be embarrassed to take one. So many of the channels in the swamp look alike, you can still get lost even with a map. Ed finished handing out the maps and opened a used cardboard box with about a dozen horns. He started handing them out to eager hands.

I continued, "We've tried to lay out the search routes close enough so if one of you gets into trouble you'll be close

171

enough for the next boat over to hear ."

A train whistle pierced the afternoon. Ed jumped up onto the platform and said, "What the hell. There's no train due in here this time'a day."

Rob's Story Continued:

"He's passed out again, Robby." Katie returned to the cab from the engine compartment. Her eyes were brimmed in tears. "I'm afraid he's dying." "We can't let him die!" I slammed the diesel's throttle all the way forward. I'll get him to your dad in time. Let the town know we're coming."

Katie braced herself and grabbed the whistle rope and pulled. She pulled on it continuously all the way into Newton. The train teetered precariously through its final turn on the outskirts of town. The crowd must'a been shocked at this black monster roaring down on them. Somebody screamed and I saw people scattering in all directions off of the track.

The train was going too fast and I didn't have time to pump the brakes. I yanked back the throttle to neutral and stepped off the deadman's switch. The roar of the diesel was replaced with a thunderous screech of tons of metal-on-metal. Katie and I was slammed off our feet and slid in a heap to the front of the cab.

Dr. Newton's Story Continued:

Ed and I stood paralyzed on the platform watching the train skidding and screeching the last quarter mile into the station.

"Harold, there's no engineer aboard that train!" Ed yelled into my ear.

I asked, "Are you sure?" I squinted through the front window of the diesel skidding closer and closer.
"There's no train scheduled for Newton until Friday."

He swung around and looked down the track. "Good Lord!" He yelled, "The track ends a block from here."

"That train's never gonna stop in time. It's gonna crash

through the barricade."

His voice was now mostly drowned out by the screeching cacophony.

I screamed, "Two people just climbed into view in the cab. It looks like a man helping a woman to her feet."

The train roared past.

Ed McKinley and I stood rooted to the platform. "Oh, my God!" We were stunned to see a young man and woman raise into view behind the front window. The young woman's blond hair swirled about her head. "Oh, my God," I repeated.

The couple waved at us and then turned and looked horrified at the barricade rushing toward them.

"Ed, that was my girl and your boy." I gasped.

Ed McKinley grasped my biceps and squeezed.

Rob's Story Continued:

"Brace yourself, Katie." I threw an arm around her and grabbed a handhold on the other side. The train slammed through the barricade and sent chunks of wood and splinters flying in all directions. The noise of screeching metal deafened our ears. We came to a stop. I looked out the window and saw we were just a few feet from the end of the track. I turned off the engine and a deep moan bellowed from the bowels of the diesel as it reluctantly died.

Dr. Newton's Story Continued:

Ed McKinley and I, along with most of the town, ran to the engine.

"Do you see them?" I asked Ed.

I didn't get an answer. Ed ran ahead and grabbed a rail and bounded aboard. He crashed through the cab's door and found the cab empty. He looked in all directions and saw a rear door swinging open. He slammed through it, stopped and gasped. Katie was cradling a huge man's head in her lap. The man's striped engineer's overalls were stained blood-red from the waist

173

down. Ed's son was trying to open an outside door and Epidus was facing Ed on her haunches with a low guttural growl -claws dug into the floor.

"What in hell?" Ed whispered.

Epidus leaped into his arms.

I, along with the rest of the town, was beside the diesel when the side door slammed open. I held it open as Ed shoved through sideways with a man as big as himself in his arms. He handed the man down to several townspeople, turned, and swallowed his son in an embrace.

"Katherine!" I hollered.

Katie bounced down the steps and threw herself at me. I grabbed her up in both arms and kissed her repeatedly.

Rob and his dad walked over to us. I looked over Katie's head at them. I released my right hand from Katie and gave Rob a Fort Pulaski salute. He snapped to attention and returned it.

I'll tell you, there wasn't a dry eye in Newton that afternoon.

Suddenly, Katie pulled back from me. "Daddy, you've got to save Smokey!"

CHAPTER 28
Rob's Story Six Months Later:

I was in full dress uniform when the Greyhound bus pulled into Clancy. I was home on summer leave. I was more than a little nervous and took off my cap and hand-brushed my crewcut while looking out the window. I saw Dad's pickup first and did a double-take; it was clean and painted.

I bounded down the steps before the bus had even come to a complete stop. The driver grinned at me and opened the door. There stood Dad and Katie. I dropped my satchel on the ground and grabbed an arm around each of them and hugged.

After a bit, Katie leaned back and said, "Rob, I've never seen you in uniform. You're as handsome as Elvis Presley!"

I smiled. "And you're still my blond-haired angel come down to bless us less fortunates." She was dressed in a white dress as frothy as high-tide covered in a print of pink roses.

Dad laughed and grabbed up my satchel. "Come on, we're holdin' a party at our house in your honor in a couple of hours."

He threw my satchel in the pickup truck bed and we climbed in-Katie in the middle. I noted a new seat cover.

"Who all is coming to my party?"

Dad shifted into second. "Katie's parents, Eloise and

175

Smokey."

Katie added, "Buffy and Epidus too."

I pinched Katie's elbow and asked Dad, "How's Smokey doing?"

"I told you in my letter Eloise was nursin' him back to health at her house. He's as good as new now." He looked over at me and grinned. "I wouldn't be surprised none if they up and got hitched one of these days. How was it for you when you got back to the soldier school?"

"It was great. Katie's Dad had blown the whistle on Major Swagart to the Academy's Board. They booted him out of there so quick the door didn't even hit him in the butt. Captain Tutin was made the new Officer-in-Charge."

Dad's pickup was kicking up a cloud of dust behind us as we bounced along the rutted road. "What finally happened to Luke?" I asked. Katie squeezed my hand. "I wrote you Sheriff Gates caught him."

"Yeah, but how?"

"After you de-coupled the engine, the rest of the train coasted to a stop and Luke skiddadled back into the swamp. I gave Sheriff Gates your map of where Luke lived and he got a posse together. They were waiting for Luke when he poled in with Larry Zitterkoph's still tank in his flat-bottom."

Dad said, "He's back in prison. His murder trial is comin' up in a few weeks."

Preacher Hatchett's old Ford was about to pass us from the other direction. Dad and the preacher waved at each other. I said, "Wasn't that Billy Crafton in the passenger seat?"

The preacher's takin' care of Billy for the next two years until Billy's daddy gets outta the caboose."

I glanced at Katie. Neither dad or her had written me anything about the moonshine trial. Katie caught my glance and straightened up in the seat. "Daddy was totally humiliated; put on trial like a common criminal. It was Rusty Yates' testimony that got the charges against Daddy dropped."

My Dad pulled onto our path and we all sat quietly in our own thoughts until we pulled up in a cloud of dust in front of our house. Epidus went wild when she saw me. It didn't bother me at all that she soaked my face with her licking and covered my uniform in dog hair. Once in the house, I was amazed at how Dad had spruced it up; it was shiny clean and freshly painted. Dad set my satchel on an almost new couch and turned to me.

"You got your choice, son. Store bought chicken or catfish I done caught from your old line? Which will it be?"

"Oh, I don't care," I said.

Katie interrupted, "Rob, why don't we show these folks just how good we cook together?"

"Like we cooked for Luke in the swamp?"

Katie smiled and nodded.

I said, "Then, it'll be catfish and hushpuppies."

Eloise and Smokey arrived carrying a hot Townsend Cake just as I was finishing filleting the fish and Katie was shaping the hushpuppies. Smokey grabbed me up in a bear hug. "I never had a proper chance to show my appreciation for you savin' my life!" he laughed. "Although you scared the gizzard outta my buddy, Ralph Welter, when he found his train gone over in Smithtown."

When Smokey set me down, Eloise took me by the hand and we walked out by the river with Ep'. We talked private conversation awhile and then Eloise commented, "Rob, you sound right educated in your talk."

"Thank's, Eloise. I'm working at improving my grammar and my grades. I'm hoping to get a scholarship when I'm finished at the Academy."

"I'm right proud of you, Robby." She gave me a private hug.

"How is your Katie doin'?

"She's going to high school up in Atlanta next year and from there, on to Smith College." I kicked my foot in the red dust. "We have growing up to do before we make lifetime decisions."

Eloise nodded and hugged me again. We looked up as Dr. Newton's Buick pulled up. We walked over and greeted the doctor and his wife. Buffy hopped out of the car and gave me a growl.

Once we all sat down for dinner, Smokey said, "Let's drink a toast to these two fine young people." He waved a small bottle around and gave us his beautiful homely smile.

"Don't mind if I do," Dr. Newton said. "And let's also toast our new plant manager as well, Ed McKinley!" He picked up a paper cup and waved it at my dad. "How 'bout it, Ed?"

Dad smiled and poured himself a glass of water. "I'll toast with this," he said. "I don't touch the hard stuff no more."

"Why not?" Smokey asked.

"Cause I don't never want nobody callin' my boy the son of a drunken' Florida Cracker again," Dad smiled.

Moonshine Express

Rod Norville